MRS PETTIGREW SEES A GHOST

MRS PETTIGREW SEES A GHOST

CHARITY SHOP HAUNTED MYSTERY BOOK ONE

KATHERINE HAYTON

Cover Design by kathay1973

ISBN: 978-0-9951007-3-2

CHAPTER ONE

*E*mily Curtis ducked her head as Pete Galveston led her out of the storefront into a narrow corridor out the back. The charity shop building was old, from the turn of the century, and people must have been shorter at the time. She was only five foot five, but the ceiling felt dangerously close to the top of her head.

"You're okay with stairs?" Pete turned with a frown of concern on his face, making Emily feel about a hundred years old.

"I'm fine with them," she insisted, waving him forward. "Not a problem."

The reply came easily to her lips, but it was a lie. Everything she used to do without giving a second thought now presented a problem. Just the short walk from the car to the charity shop door had set off an ache deep in her right hip. By the end of the day, the dull pain would grow into a set of teeth, gnawing on her bones.

But Emily had never been one to burden someone else with her problems.

"How long have you worked here?" she asked, trying

not to breathe too heavily as she navigated the steep staircase. "I don't remember the store from the last time I was in town."

Pete gave a short bark of laughter. "Then you haven't been in town for a long time. I've been working here for eight years but it was around long before that." He pulled at the rainbow-coloured suspenders holding up his dark crimson jeans. "We've been on the main street all that time."

Emily shrugged an apology and Pete unlocked the door at the top of the stairs, opening it to reveal a flurry of dust particles dancing in a beam of sunlight. "Here we are."

Where the downstairs held the scents of damp wool and old leather-bound books, upstairs the room smelled of patchouli and lavender. Perhaps Pete noticed the wrinkle of Emily's nose because he gave another of his strange laughs. "It's from incense. The last woman we had working up here enjoyed lighting a cone every other day."

Emily nodded as she edged into the room, taking everything in slowly. Since the car accident, her eyes weren't as reliable as they'd once been. Nothing was. She looked at every item, fixing on the odds and ends until they formed into a complete picture.

The sunlight streamed in from a dormer window, cut into the slope of the roof. Old wooden floorboards, worn free of varnish, were set with gaps between them wide enough to lose a coin. A coatstand lurked in the corner of the room. Plastic supermarket bags stuffed full of old clothing and knick-knacks hung from each bronze hook, the sheen of metal lost to greening.

Elsewhere, boxes took up most of the space. Cardboard boxes held together with brown masking tape sat atop wooden crates. Heavy plastic containers rested on the floor, sitting cheek to jowl with rusted metal trunks.

An elegantly carved wooden chest caught Emily's attention, and she ventured forward, caressing the chestnut protected with a sheen of varnish. Beautiful.

"That came in this morning," Pete said with a nod. "You'll need to go out to the house today to collect the rest of the belongings. We like to make a move on these things quickly. Otherwise, it distresses the family and they might change their minds."

"Will there be much more?" Emily turned a concerned glance in his direction. "I've only got a Suzuki hatchback." Once upon a time, she'd had a snazzy BMW Boxster with even less space than now. She'd traded down, taking part of the insurance in a cash settlement. The thought of her old car raised a lump in her throat for more reasons than one.

"The housekeeper assured me it was just another few boxes. You can always make a couple of trips if there's too many."

She nodded, forcing a smile to her lips to hide her worry over what that short sentence might mean. Her hip gave another dull groan, reminding her of the new physical limitations.

"Did they give you a preferred time?"

"Here," he held out a small card. "I've written it all down for you."

Emily hesitated, blushing at her impediment. "Did the agency tell you I have limitations?"

"Oh, right." Pete put the note back in his pocket. "Sorry, I forgot. The house is at the end of Barbell Lane—do you know the place?"

"Is that the one that intersects beside the tearooms?"

"That's it. Follow it right down to the end, past the

creek, and there's a double-storied villa, red brick and ivy. That's them. After ten o'clock, the housekeeper said."

"Okay."

"You shouldn't feel embarrassed, you know. We've all got problems." Pete ran his fingers through the four-inch beard, which sat below a bushy moustache—the twirled ends gleaming with wax. The extravagant facial hair didn't cover the impact of his meth-damaged teeth. "I didn't see myself ending up here, either. You have to do the best you can with what you have."

The bell from the front door of the charity shop tinkled, drawing Pete's attention. "I'll be back in a minute. Have a good look around."

He ran down the steps with an ease that made a lump rise in Emily's throat. In the long months since a truck broadsided her at the intersection of Harewood and Greers Road, she'd often given in to self-pity. It wasn't an attractive feature but as her injuries forced her to give up one thing after another, it was a habit she found hard to break.

Her eyes caught their reflection in a tarnished mirror, suspended on an oak frame. The silver curls still took Emily by surprise, even though she'd removed her first white hair with a cry of disgust at twenty-seven. A good twenty-five years had passed since then.

Somehow, the process of aging had taken place without drawing her attention. Now, she was an old woman. A useless old woman. Without thinking, her fingers crept up to her forehead to trace the puckered lines of her scar across her brow and down her cheek.

With a shake of her head, Emily backed away and forced her thoughts back to the task in hand. She opened the wooden chest, searching for a distraction. On top of the items was an embroidered sachet. She raised it up to her nose, breathing in the aroma of sandalwood and vanilla.

When she'd been a young girl, her mother made similar sachets for Emily to store in her underwear drawer. Like the wallpaper lining she'd replaced every springtime, it was a ritual that had disappeared over the years. Nostalgia rose in a bubble, tightening her chest.

Underneath lay a set of napkins. The delicate needle-work formed a different pattern on each, detailing a variety of forest wildlife in cream stitching on heavy cream fabric. The pieces were rolled and crimped as though recently removed from napkin holders.

Emily supposed the holders must be far more expensive —sterling silver or gold leaf—but her heart wished she could see them. Even if it was only to take a glimpse before handing them back to the family.

At the back of the chest was a painting. She pulled it out, having to insert her fingers along the front to remove it without jerking.

Before Emily turned it over to verify the artist, she knew Maurice Detrere had painted the portrait. The precise brush strokes formed as much a part of his signature as the thumbprint and name scrawled on the back.

"Found something interesting already?"

Emily jumped. She'd been lost so deep in her own thoughts she'd missed Pete's tread on the stairs. "This painting is by a good artist." She turned it around for him to see. "It's a pity it won't fetch much at auction."

Her new job entailed searching through the deceased estates gifted to the charity shop and identifying and selling high-value items through private or public auction. Rather than pay a wage, the role granted her commission of ten percent on each successful sale.

"Why not?" Pete moved closer, squinting at the woman's image captured in the rich oils.

"Portraits never do." Emily stared at the painting, feeling a pang of loss. Maurice Detrere had captured an expression of quiet sadness enveloped in a strong dignity.

A beautiful woman but unsatisfied.

"They only mean something to the family or friends who knew the model, unless it's the Mona Lisa. No matter how talented the artist, nobody wants to bid top dollar to have a stranger's image hanging on their wall."

She looked back at the wooden chest. The other contents were kitchen or dining room items. As well as the embroidered napkins, there were enamel milk jugs, a china tea set, and a huge collection of crockery. The painting didn't fit in with the other treasures.

"I wonder if they intended for us to receive this." Emily moved back to the chest, stroking along the handle of a striped teacup. "They might've placed it in here by accident."

"What about the gold frame?" Pete edged closer, his eyes still fixed on the painting. "Is that worth anything?"

"No. It's been replaced." Emily held the picture out again, pointing to the line of discolouration along the backing. "I imagine the original was in keeping with the price of the commission, but this is just gold paint on wood. It doesn't even fit."

Pete clapped his hands together. "Take it back, then. You can ask the family when you're picking up the next load of stuff. We don't need anything stored up here that won't sell. It's hard enough to turn over the goods we have downstairs as it is."

Emily nodded, leaning the painting against the side wall. It slid further down, the sudden movement making it appear as though the woman in the image had jumped. She gave it a hard stare, then readjusted it so the portrait faced the wall.

"Good idea," Pete said, moving over to a cardboard box with a determined expression on his face and a box cutter in his hand. "You don't want someone looking at you while you're trying to work."

CHAPTER TWO

*P*inetar township might have gained a charity shop on its main street since Emily left as a teenager to attend university, but little else had changed. The road through the centre of town still didn't present much of an obstacle for visitors or residents crossing against the lights. The tearooms still had an honesty box next to the till for when the manageress took her breaks.

Best of all, the drive to the end of Barbell Road took Emily into the oldest part of town. Houses built at the turn of the century when Pinetar fancied itself an important trading post and rest stop on the long trek out of Christchurch.

The old villas stretched out with long verandas built to take advantage of summer heat that didn't get started until February, then was over in a snap. Grapevines weaved through the carved roof supports—a variety found throughout the Canterbury region with purple fruit, tart, and packed as much full of seeds as juice.

Trees in this suburb—the streets wide enough to take a dual horse carriage and let it turn around without trouble—

were well established and sourced straight from good old England. The colonialists who planted them had razed the native Kauri and Totara to make way for the imported Oaks and Weeping Willows. Given the median age at the time, the men must have died long before their handiwork bore fruit.

The sturdier brick houses were lovely to look at and disastrous to use. Working from plans drawn up in a country on the other side of the world, in New Zealand they captured shadows instead of the sun, turning their residents paler and colder than the upper classes they'd left back home.

Still, the addition of skylights and double glazing had taken care of those problems in recent decades. The heat pump vents might blemish the brickwork, but they drew the damp out of the wooden fittings and eradicated a century of endemic mould.

Emily pulled the car up alongside the creek and walked over to the fence meant to protect little children from succumbing to its liquid embrace. As she leaned on the rickety edge, doubting it would stop an adventurous toddler, a cooling breeze lifted the grey curls away from her forehead.

Watercress and weeds flourished along the sides of the creek bed. The trickle of water at the base of such luxuriousness was a disappointment. Only a surging river could have done the plenitude of greenery justice.

A long time ago, she'd played on those banks during the long school break over summer. She'd placed her shoes on the footpath, socks rolled into balls inside, before charging down to sink her toes into the mud.

The dim light piercing through the intertwining branches overhead had always felt like a shelter built especially for children. Under the lush foliage, you couldn't hear your mother calling out to come and help her with supper or hang out the washing. Ignorance was the perfect excuse.

For a brief second, Emily fought the urge to take her shoes off and plunge down the bank without delay. It was her hip rather than common sense that stopped her. A twinge as the muscle cried out for a better blood supply. Going downhill posed its own problems but it would be nothing compared to the Herculean effort of having to clamber back up to the roadside.

"The time is ten o'clock," Emily's watch announced. Without the ability to read numbers or words any longer, robotic voices had become her steadfast companions.

It was a short walk to the front door, then she hesitated, steeling herself for the grief that would be written over the family's faces. A husband and son, Pete had told her, along with a gardener and housekeeper who'd been with them for decades.

Emily pressed a hand against her stomach to steady it, then knocked on the door. Enough time passed that she was about to try again when footsteps approached. A woman answered her knock, aged in her sixties, grey hair pulled back in a bun.

"Hello," Emily said with a compassionate smile, "I'm from the charity shop. I've come to collect the rest of Mrs Pettigrew's belongings."

The woman gave a curt nod and stepped back, waving Emily indoors. "They're all packed up, ready to go. Through here."

She led the way to a side room, which looked to be a storeroom judging from the dimness, the swollen creak of the door, and the dust. A trail marked where the chest already delivered to the shop had been dragged, twin lines showing where the rounded feet had touched the floor.

Emily stared in confusion at the mountain of boxes. "Is all of this to go?"

"Well, it can't stay here." The housekeeper turned and looked at Emily askance. "I told the lad at the charity shop, I couldn't handle bringing it all down to him. He assured me you guys could handle it."

"Of course." Emily gave a determined nod and stepped into the airless room. "I'll just need to make a few more trips than I thought." She grabbed hold of the box nearest her and lifted. It weighed ten kilos or more and her back demanded she immediately drop it back onto the floor. "I don't suppose you have a trolley or something, do you?"

"How old are you, love?"

"Fifty-two. I'll be fine once I get started, I'm sure."

The woman didn't answer, just snorted. "Hang on a minute." She walked away, her rubber soles squeaking on the polished floorboards. Emily's heart pounded in her chest, though whether from the short exertion or the strange atmosphere of the house, she couldn't decide.

At the base of the main staircase, the woman stopped and yelled, "Gregory, get down here. We need a hand moving your mum's boxes."

"Oh, are you sure?" Emily stepped out of the room, picking at the loose skin of her throat. "I don't mean to disturb—"

"He does nothing else. About time we got him to lend a hand doing something useful." The housekeeper gave a sniff and moved up one step. "Gregory! I said to get down here. I'm not going to stand here yelling all day long."

A door slammed up above and the woman turned, a satisfied smile on her face. "I'll stick around to direct operations if you don't mind. Otherwise, the lad'll just slink off back into his bedroom to play on his console. Lazy as sin, he is."

"I suppose if his mother's just—"

"Always been that way," the woman said, sweeping past Emily to stand at the doorway to the storage room. "From the moment he was born. Couldn't even be bothered to cry out when he was hungry. Just waited around until someone remembered to check."

A man in his early twenties slunk down the staircase, his feet barely making a sound. The housekeeper gave an exasperated sigh. "Put your shoes on, Gregory. Her car's not parked inside the house."

Emily just had time enough to glimpse a flapping blond fringe above bloodshot hazel eyes, then the lad turned and began the laborious task of walking back upstairs.

"He'll be an age. You want a cup of tea while you're waiting?"

The woman didn't stay long enough for her to answer, trotting off toward a room on the other side of the house instead. After a moment of hesitation, Emily followed along, shooting a glance up the massive staircase.

"My name's Hilda Mainstrop," the housekeeper said as Emily took a seat in the light and airy room. Judging from the spacious windows, the kitchen was a late addition to the house. A suspended pot rack hanging above the marble-top bench offset the high ceiling.

"I'm Emily Curtis."

"You new in town?"

Emily nodded. "I arrived back a few weeks ago. My parents lived here for a while when I was younger, but I haven't been back since I was a teen."

"Happens a lot around here," Hilda mused. "The young

ones go off to study for their degrees and never come back. Only the ones too lazy to do that stick around, and who wants that?"

Not knowing what the correct answer was, Emily stayed silent. She presumed the speech was another dig at the young man upstairs but, without knowing him personally, it felt rude to join in the attack on his character.

"Have you been working for the Pettigrew's a long time?" she asked instead, already knowing the answer courtesy of Pete.

"Since I was in my early forties." Hilda lifted the kettle, ready to pour the hot water over the tea leaves, then stopped. Her face blanked of expression as she stared out into the side garden.

"It must be nice to have a career with the same employer all that time." Emily shifted on her seat, remembering her own role as an accountant. She'd joined the firm straight out of university, working her way up to become a managing partner. Now she couldn't even recognise numbers, let alone tally them.

Hilda shook herself and gave another derisive snort. "It's not like I have a choice. Work's short around here unless you're into farming. I suppose I was lucky to get a job doing the same stuff my husband always expected me to do for free, but it rarely feels like it."

"But Mrs Pettigrew treated you well?"

"Hardly." The housekeeper began wiping down the countertop with furious strokes. "She didn't even like me to take sick days, and they're government regulated. A few months ago, I got terrible vertigo and she just said I could sit on a chair to clean."

Emily clenched her hands together, feeling out of kilter.

"I guess at our age, at least retirement's just around the corner."

Although she presented the information as though it was a relief, Emily couldn't stand the thought of not having a job. Even with her brain injury, the Protestant work ethic that had prodded her conscience out of bed since her first day of work was still on duty.

Again, Hilda shook her head. "*Some* of us can't afford to do that. The superannuation will come in handy on top of my income but giving up work's a long sight further off than that."

Emily decided keeping her mouth shut might be a better choice. In a minute, Hilda placed a cup of tea in her hand and that ended her compulsive need to converse.

"What're you doing in here?" Gregory slouched against the door to the kitchen, looking aggrieved. "I thought you wanted to move boxes."

"It'll be a great help," Emily gushed, getting in her thanks before the evil twinkle in Hilda's eye could unleash a tirade. "I'm sorry about your mum."

"She wasn't my mum."

"Gregory! Cynthia looked after you for the past fifteen years. How dare you say such a thing?"

"It's the truth." Gregory jerked his head back to flick the fringe out of his eyes. "My real mum's been dead so long I can barely remember her." He stared with open curiosity at Emily, his eyes tracing the path of her scar along her forehead and down the side of her face.

She clenched hold of her teacup, refusing the urge to raise her hand up to shield the damage. If the teenager wanted to be rude and stare, let him. It was long past time she stopped feeling embarrassed by the twisting line of healing tissue.

"How did Mrs Pettigrew die?" she asked, then bit her lip hard. *None of your business,* she reprimanded herself before anyone else got the chance.

But Gregory didn't appear bothered by the question. Instead, his eyes lit up with delight. "Head injury," he said, licking his lips after the statement. "Her skull just burst open like a ripe tomato."

"Get into the storeroom," Hilda exploded, her cheeks bursting into flame. She slammed her cup into the saucer with such force it cracked. "Try helping someone out for once in your life."

She pulled a tea towel from the oven handle, twisting it around her hand. The young man's eyes widened, and he backed out of the room. Emily stood and followed him a moment later, not wanting to stay in the same place as such fury.

"My car's parked out by the creek," she said as she walked into the storeroom. "I'll carry a box and lead the way."

"Don't be silly." Gregory's face was pale apart from a blotch of colour high on each cheek. "The last thing I need is that old witch coming in here raging because you strained your back lifting something. Just hold the doors open and I'll sort out the rest."

She did as he asked, holding the entrance open until he'd passed through with two boxes stacked on top of each other. Just watching the muscles on the young man's arms working made Emily glad she'd left the job to him.

Once he was clear of the front door, she hurried ahead —Ignoring the gnashing teeth in her hip to get to the car before Gregory did. With a double beep, the rear unlocked, and Emily lifted the hatchback door.

The boxes didn't fit at first, but the boy manhandled

them, crushing the tops and sides until the door could slam down and click.

"I hope there's nothing too expensive in there," she said with a smile, but Gregory just scowled back at her.

She opened the passenger side door, where they might fit another box and the boy jerked back, his eyes widening. While Emily stared on in confusion, he opened his mouth and screamed.

CHAPTER THREE

"I'm so sorry," Emily said as Hilda helped her move Gregory to a chair. The boy's weight had almost collapsed her on the trip back from the car and his legs folded as soon as his rear end perched above the seat. "I forgot all about the painting."

"The silly boy's just putting on a show." Hilda's mouth twisted into a sneer. She clicked her fingers underneath Gregory's nose. "Come on, lad. Wakey-wakey."

He roused enough to push her hand away, but Emily saw the sheen of tears in his eyes. For all his play-act at not caring earlier, it appeared his stepmother's death had affected him. If the circumstances had been different, she'd have been relieved.

"Why d'you bring that horrid thing back here, anyway?"

Emily turned to Hilda with a gasp of surprise. "It's a lovely painting. I thought someone might've put it in the chest by mistake." She chewed her lip as the housekeeper stared back at her impassively. "Often people like to hold onto portraits as a reminder."

"Not that one." Hilda sounded adamant. "I swear, the

eyes follow you around the room. It used to be up in the master's study and every month I went in there to dust, she'd stare at me like I was doing something wrong."

"She looked sad to me," Emily said, remembering the hint of despair trapped in the oil painting's eyes. "Mrs Pettigrew was a beautiful woman."

"To look at, maybe."

Gregory gave a gasp and Emily stepped forward, hand out to steady him. He shook his head, closing his eyes. "When we read Dorian Gray at school, I tried to get into Dad's study for a week to see if the same held true for Cynthia."

"Don't call her that." Hilda put her hands on her hips. "Show some respect."

"She's dead. She doesn't need my respect." Gregory met the elder woman's eyes for a moment, then his fell to the floor. "Fine. I thought my *step*mother's painting would be all haggard and ugly."

"I didn't mean to startle anyone." Emily's hands wrung together no matter how much she tried to force them to her sides. "I just needed to verify it hadn't gone out by mistake."

"Don't you worry." Hilda put a hand on Emily's shoulder. "You did a nice thing, bringing it down here to check. It's not your fault the younger generation is made of jelly. How about you take the loaded boxes back to the shop and I'll see if I can scare up Abraham Greening to give you a hand instead?"

At Emily's blank look she explained, "He's the gardener."

"That'd be lovely." Emily backed up to the door and had to resist the urge to run as soon as she stepped outside the house. The sun's rays already had power behind them, and she wondered how hot the loft at the charity shop would get by the end of the day.

"I CAN GET the next load if you like," Pete offered when Emily recounted her morning. "If you stay here and watch the till..."

He trailed off, presumably remembering she couldn't handle that task, and Emily said, "I'm happy to go back. I was just making idle chit-chat. The whole family struck me as odd, but it's no bother."

"We see all sorts in here," Pete said with a gap-toothed smile. "And you never can tell how death will affect someone. Chances are if you went back in a few weeks, they'd be different."

"I suppose so." Emily felt her lip turning down at the corners and forced a smile back into place. "Anyway, the housekeeper said the gardener would help out with the next load so at least it won't be someone so close."

When she pulled up next to the house this time, a stack of boxes sat on the curb, ready to go. Emily maneuvered them into the back of the car, not seeing anyone. With the new load on board, she drove back to the shop and unpacked.

By the time she got the new boxes upstairs, Emily had forgotten the ache in her hip. A shrieking pain in her shoulders had overtaken it.

Another journey, there and back, and the dream of a hot bath took up the forefront of her mind. The next round-trip, the gardener was standing on the curbside next to the load, twisting a leather hat in his hands. He was a lot younger than she'd expected, maybe mid-thirties but no older. As her eyes swept across his wide-set eyes and strong jaw, she registered he was handsome, too.

"Is this the last of them?" Emily asked, pulling herself out of the car by the roof handle. She gritted her teeth to stop limping as she walked over to him. "There's been quite a lot."

"Yeah. That's all of them, now."

He stood still, not moving to help as Emily bent to heft up the box while fumbling the hatch open. As the weight inside the carton moved, it slipped out of her grip. The gardener leapt forward to catch it a moment before it fell to the ground.

"Whoopsie-daisy. I'll load that into the back if you like." He pushed in the first and turned around to hook the second up with one arm, making Emily feel even more useless.

"I just wanted to catch you before you went," he said, stepping back to the safety of the curb again. "See, I wanted to ask you to take good care of her things. She put a lot of effort into collecting all those antiques, you know."

"Is there anything you wanted to grab out of here before I go?" Emily felt for the man who looked utterly bereft.

He scratched the back of his neck as he stared over his shoulder at the house. "Nah. I'd better be getting back to it. I wanted to check the ladyship's possessions were going to a good home."

The ladyship?

"I'll take good care while they're in the shop and I'm sure whoever ends up with them will treasure the items."

"Mm." The man shook himself, then popped the twisted hat on his head. "That's good to hear. She was a special lady, Mrs Pettigrew. Very special, indeed."

Emily smiled and held onto the car door for support,

uncertain what else she could say. After an awkward silence, the gardener nodded as though she'd just said a final goodbye. "I'll be seeing you, then."

He turned and crunched up the gravel driveway, splitting off the main path to walk around the back of the house, and out of sight.

IF EMILY's mother had lower standards when raising her, she would have cursed under her breath as she pulled up outside the local rehabilitation centre.

Although every muscle in her body informed her loud and clear she'd worked out more than enough for one day, Emily still forced herself to walk into the session. It had taken her too long to find the physio to just blow off an appointment due to being tired.

"You seem stiffer than last week," Joanne Ardue commented as they worked through the routine. She smelled of musk and spice, like the Tabac deodorant one of Emily's beaus had used a long time ago. A *very* long time ago. "Has something happened?"

"I started my new job," Emily admitted after a short inner tussle. She lifted a medicine ball, the piece of equipment she hated most in the gym. Already, her arms trembled, and the ball eased too far to her left side. She squatted, her knees popping with such an alarming crack they sounded like they'd broken clean in two.

"Doing what? Manual labour?" Joanne frowned while Emily tried to remember which muscles would get her back to a standing position.

"I just lifted a few boxes."

"Okay. Take my hand."

Emily ignored the offer for a moment, then sighed and grabbed hold. Joanne lifted her to her feet.

"I've warned you before about overtaxing yourself. It might seem like the quickest way to return to your full physical fitness, but it's far more likely you'll end up doing permanent damage."

"Yes, Miss." Emily hung her head, biting onto her lower lip to stop the sudden well of rage that bubbled up inside her. This *girl* was half her age, maybe not even that. To think she had the temerity to *lecture* a woman of years.

"And don't pull that passive-aggressive nonsense, either," Joanne continued with a frown. "You're better than that. Owning your recovery means owning your mistakes as well."

The rage seeped away again as soon as it had come. "I'm sorry." Emily raised a hand to comb her hair back from her eyes and was appalled at how much it shook. She lowered it to her side again, hiding the evidence. "This is just turning into a terrible day."

But Joanne didn't accept the excuse. Her bull-headedness had been part of the reason Emily chose her. "Next time, stop it becoming a bad day by asking for help when you're asked to do something outside your physical comfort zone. It's okay to push yourself in here, with my supervision, but do it out in the real world and it could turn nasty."

Emily accepted the reprimand with a nod. "It was my first day, so I wasn't sure what to expect. I'll ask for help in the future."

The lie, meant to appease Joanne, worked better on herself.

"How is it?" the physio asked. "Being back at work?"

"It's nice to be around people again. Even though I see you every week and the doctor once a month, I miss having people in my life. I thought about getting a pet to help with the loneliness, but my neurologist said it would be too much responsibility."

Joanne smiled. "Did he tell you to start off with a plant and work your way up from there?"

Emily frowned and shook her head. "No. Why? Is that something you recommend?"

"It's the advice given to people in addiction recovery to avoid stressing themselves out with too much too quickly."

"I'm not an addict!" Emily drew back, appalled.

"Not saying you were, just that the advice might be sensible for you too. Start off small and work your way up. It's easier to remember to water a plant once a week than feed and water a pet every single day."

In the car, Emily traced the scar along her face, pushing at the skin as though she could mould it back into its original shape. When she grew tired, it throbbed, but her fingertips probably caused more damage than good. With a sigh, she dropped her hand to the wheel and headed for home.

Even though the session had wiped her out, Emily still pulled out a pad to practice her numbers and letters. When the truck's front wheels had crushed her head inside the twisted metal wreckage of her little BMW boxster, a skull fragment had pierced straight into the zone where her brain processed written language.

She could talk, she could listen, but show her a page of written words and Emily might as well have been reading an ancient, unknowable alphabet.

The mathematical symbols that had defined her career as an accountant were a messy jumble without meaning. Although her physical limitations annoyed Emily, this was the heart and soul of her vexation.

Numbers formed her identity. Without them, she no longer knew who to be.

Each night, she practised, hoping the stars would align and this time—*this time*—the recognition might come flooding back. With painstaking attention, Emily traced out each digit, each letter, copying them from a cardboard backed child's book.

With diligence, she stared at each copied shape, willing the memory of the number into her mind. Each blink eroded the knowledge, the digits turning back into meaningless squiggles and lines.

Enough!

Emily tossed the pad aside and lay back on her bed, eyes, mind, and body reeling from the long day. The image of Gregory's shocked face popped up, bringing a glut of guilt along with it. The poor kid, seeing his stepmother's likeness sitting in her passenger seat. She could only hope she hadn't scarred him for life.

Given Hilda's scathing attitude toward him, he probably had too thick a skin for that, but still.

Thinking of the odd mixture of people she'd met earlier in the day, Emily drifted off to sleep.

———

A LOW HUM roused Emily from her slumber. As her mind rose through the layers of consciousness, she first thought it was her mother singing to her in her crib. She opened her eyes, still unused to the angles and windows of the bedroom she'd slept in for the past few weeks.

"Hm," a low voice whispered in her ear. It rose another few notes. "Tra-la-la."

Emily sat bolt upright in bed. Her heart froze mid-beat,

then hammered at her chest like she was the last nail to be pounded in before quitting time.

A woman stood beside the bed, staring at her.

Emily tossed aside the covers and struggled to her feet. Her leg buckled, spilling her back onto the mattress. She gasped and pushed herself back to a standing position with her hands.

"Who are you?" she asked while feeling for her dressing gown. She slipped it on, a protective layer against the intruder. "What are you doing in my bedroom?"

"I might ask you the same thing." The woman placed her hands on her hips and jutted out her chin. "I've no idea what I'm doing in this tiny little box, but I can assure you, if you don't take me home at once you'll live to regret it!"

The woman spoke in the plummy tones of a newsreader from the 1960s. Her hairstyle was similar, coiffed on top of her head and bedecked with pearls, although she couldn't be more than forty.

It triggered a memory but, in her shock, Emily couldn't place it.

She needed to get into the hallway and make a break for her front door. The neighbours, Mr and Mrs Huntaway, would rouse from sleep if she yelled loud enough. They'd come to her aid, with the husband bringing along his biggest butcher's knife while he was at it.

The thought of the woman facing something as fearful as what Emily faced now lent her enough energy to make the short dash to the door. She pulled on the handle, losing her balance and falling to one knee.

"Oh, dear. Are you all right?" The woman drifted over to Emily's side and bent over, a concerned expression on her face. "You won't be able to drive me home if you hurt yourself. Should you be moving at that pace at your age?"

The insult spurred Emily into a rage. She spun, poking her finger at the woman's face. "How dare you? I'm perfectly capable. Now, you get out of my house and don't come back unless you want to face my rifle."

"Your rifle?" The woman sniggered. "Since you can't even open the door without falling over, I dare say no one would allow you to own a firearm." She tilted her head to one side, her right eyebrow arched. "Do they even let old age pensioners have a gun licence?"

"I'm not a pensioner! I'm barely into my fifties."

Emily ran a hand through her hair, screwing her eyes up in concentration. The conversation had gone so far off track she didn't know if she was coming or going. "How long have you been in here, watching me sleeping?"

"Not long. I can assure you if I'd spent any more than a few minutes in this airless trap, I'd be far more disagreeable."

"How d'you get in?"

The woman pulled at a loose strand of hair near her mouth, twisting it around her forefinger while she frowned. "I don't know. I can remember watching my soaps on television, then I was here."

With a start, Emily realised the retirement village was just a few hundred metres along the street. The hospital section catered mostly for the elderly but always had a few others in their care. Alzheimer's patients, for instance.

That must be it. A woman with a case of early-onset dementia who'd wandered away and couldn't remember.

The explanation relaxed her. Emily could cope with a patient, especially one so slight of build. She'd take her arm and guide her back to where she should be, just as soon as she got dressed.

"Why don't you wait outside the room for a minute?"

Emily cooed in as reassuring a voice as she could manage. "I'll get dressed and drive you back home if you give me a second to get myself decent."

The woman gave a snort and shook her head. "It'll take a lot more than a few minutes to conjure that miracle, don't you think?"

Biting back a retort to the rude comment, Emily reached for the woman's arm to guide her out the door. As her fingers went straight through the limb and out the other side, she gave a startled cry.

The memory of where she'd seen the woman before socked home. Horror and recognition dawned at the same moment.

"You're Mrs Pettigrew," Emily said in a barely audible voice. "You're a ghost."

CHAPTER FOUR

"*J*'m not a ghost!" Mrs Pettigrew held out her hand, turning it one way then the other. "See? Solid as anything."

Emily gathered up her nerve and gave the woman a poke. Her finger travelled straight into the ghost's side, ending up somewhere in the middle of where her kidneys should be, then she pulled it back, wiping her hand against her dressing gown. "You look like you're there, but you're not."

"Rubbish." In case Emily hadn't interpreted her opinion correctly the woman also gave a large snort. "If I was a ghost, you wouldn't be able to see me at all."

"I don't know why I can." Emily frowned, wishing Mrs Pettigrew was right and she couldn't see her. Or hear her.

The moon streamed in through the window she'd left open for the light breeze, forming a silver path along the floor. Although it didn't shine straight through the ghost, Mrs Pettigrew didn't cast a shadow. Emily was about to point it out, then thought twice. Would that be rude?

"This is a tiny room." The ghost crossed her arms over

her chest and paced back and forth. "Is the rest of the house this small?"

"It's old," Emily said, trying not to let her indignation show. She had to be careful with money since the accident. Her old salary had disappeared and despite years of budget advice to strangers, she'd never set up a diligent savings plan for herself.

The ghost snorted again. "My house is old, and it's gigantic. That's hardly an excuse." Mrs Pettigrew turned and squinted at Emily. "Are you very poor? Do you think that's why I've appeared here? To help you financially?"

"I don't need any financial help and I can't see what good you'd do if I did. Unless you know where a heap of treasure is buried, what were you planning?"

"There's no need to get uppity." The woman turned away, her nose tilting into the air.

Just as Emily opened her mouth to apologise, Mrs Pettigrew caught sight of her practice letters and numbers. "What on earth are all these squiggles? This handwriting is even worse than my GP and Dr Pearson has a famously terrible hand."

Emily reached over and snatched the pad away, pressing it to her chest. "None of your business."

The ghost gave an elaborate sigh and drifted over to the window. "Oh, I know this part of town," she said with a cry of delight. "We're near to Main Street."

"Perhaps you should go there," Emily suggested. "See if something there tells you why you've appeared in my bedroom in the middle of the night."

"How did you know my name?"

Emily felt the words land on her like an accusation. She hunched her shoulders and perched on the side of the bed. "Your family donated a lot of your possessions to the charity shop where I work. I've been sorting through them."

The ghost's gaze intensified until Emily shifted her position to avoid staring straight back at her. "What possessions? You mean bits of old tat?"

"I haven't looked at all of it yet, but a lot of large boxes," Emily replied, still feeling the weight in her back and shoulders. "Along with a wooden chest."

Mrs Pettigrew held out a hand to steady herself on the windowsill. Her fingers plunged straight through the wood, leaving her off balance.

Emily jumped up to stop the woman falling, but she was no better at catching her than the sill had been. Mrs Pettigrew stumbled to her right, one leg buckling, and landed on her knee.

"There must be a mistake," she mumbled. "Why would my family give away all my treasures?"

"Well," Emily moved back a step, not wanting to crowd her. "You're a ghost, remember? They won't have need of them any longer."

"I don't feel well. Do you have a brandy I can use to settle my nerves?"

Emily shook her head. Since her accident, alcohol didn't agree with her. "I doubt you could drink it," she said in placation. "Not in your current state."

Mrs Pettigrew pursed her lips, in denial of what should have been obvious to her.

An idea occurred to Emily, and she picked up a silver backed hand mirror from her dressing table. "Why don't you have a look at yourself and I'll show you something?"

She held the mirror at an angle the ghost could see, then stretched out a finger. "Are you watching?"

"Yes, I'm watching. What is it?"

The note of annoyance gave Emily the courage to follow through with her plan. She poked her finger into the side of Mrs Pettigrew's cheek and, although the woman flinched, kept it moving until it looked like a thick kebab skewer sticking out of her head.

"Do you see?"

The ghost jerked backwards, holding her hand up in a warding off gesture. "I don't see anything. Get away from me!"

"Really? Because you look like you've seen a ghost." Judging from the knitted eyebrows on Mrs Pettigrew's face, the small joke had missed its mark.

Emily moved back a step, then laid the mirror face-up on the floor. "I'll make myself a cup of cocoa. It's far too late at night to have an esoteric discussion without something. I'll be back in a few minutes."

She hobbled toward the door, favouring her left side. Out in the corridor, she turned back to the ghost. "If you wanted to leave, now would be a good time."

Mrs Pettigrew stayed on the floor, one hand cupping her cheek and her eyes full of ghost tears. It didn't appear as if she had the energy to go anywhere.

Emily shuffled down the hallway, one painful step at a time, supposing that in similar circumstances, she might feel the same.

"Have you always been able to see ghosts?"

Emily blew on the top of her cocoa, then took a cautious sip. Perfect. Although she usually sweetened the brew with Splenda tablets, tonight she'd thrown caution to the wind and dumped in four heaped teaspoons of sugar. It wouldn't help when it came time to have another attempt at sleep, but that seemed a distant event.

"You're the first," she said after swallowing another delicious mouthful. "And, no offence, but I hope you're the last."

Mrs Pettigrew preened at the start of the sentence and ignored the latter. "It's a change to be the first for something. After spending the last fifteen years as a second wife, it's nice to break free."

"Well, I'm glad I could oblige." Emily smiled. If she'd thought such a thing could ever happen to her, she'd never have imagined the conversation going this way. She'd think of herself as the one clutching her throat, terrified, whereas the roles were now reversed.

"Do you know how I died?"

The image of Gregory flashed up in Emily's mind and she spluttered out half her mouthful. *Her head just burst open like a ripe tomato.* There was no way on earth she'd say such a thing to the ghost, no matter how rude or annoying the woman appeared on first acquaintance.

But with Mrs Pettigrew staring at her through keen eyes, Emily had to say something. "Why don't we look up the notice in the paper? I didn't want to ask your family questions about it." *Not after the information your stepson volunteered!*

"Do you keep old papers?"

Emily frowned, wondering if the ghost was joking for a moment, then deciding she didn't look the type. "No. I meant to check online."

The ghost sniffed and tilted her nose into the air. "Precise language is so important if you want to avoid being misunderstood. Although..."

She trailed off and Emily didn't want to ask her the

obvious question to get her restarted. *Although, what?* She took another big gulp of her cocoa to stop her mouth running away with the question before her mind could put a stop to it.

Mrs Pettigrew wasn't so easily put off, however. While Emily held her tongue, she waited for a beat, then continued regardless. "Your handwriting does leave a lot to be desired. I suppose you have trouble reading."

"About as much trouble as you have living."

So much for holding her tongue!

The ghost gave her a glare through narrowed eyes, then tilted her nose even farther into the air. At this rate, soon Emily would be staring straight up her nostrils. She gulped another mouthful of cocoa, then the last. It was grainy with undissolved sugar and she kept it in her mouth a second longer, letting her tongue absorb the glorious sweetness from the crystals.

"It'll just take a few minutes for my laptop to get going," she said, snagging the corner of the machine and dragging it out from under the bed. The poor device had a thick coating of dust over it. When Emily swept her arm across the top, her sleeve gained a thick taupe line.

"Didn't your mother ever teach you to take good care of your things?"

"My mother died when I was very young," Emily answered. It wasn't quite true—she'd been in her early twenties—but it felt true, nonetheless. Either way, the answer silenced Mrs Pettigrew's careless tongue, which was all she cared about for the moment.

The machine booted up and Emily leaned over the keyboard, fingers poised to type, then realised her mistake.

The computer had gathered dust because it required someone able to read and write to operate it. Her exclusion from that group was recent enough it had dropped from her mind.

As the squiggles on the keyboard appeared to squirm and writhe before her tired eyes, abject sorrow for the person she'd once been filled up Emily's mind.

"Well? What are you waiting for?"

Emily didn't want to explain herself. It was late, she'd only had an hour or two's sleep, and her body was aching from the day's exertion. "I need to rest. We can do this in the morning."

She snapped the lid back into place and lay back on the bed. As uncomfortable as it felt to have someone glaring at her while she tried to sleep, Emily kept her eyelids shut.

It would be a hundred times more uncomfortable to explain.

Tomorrow, she could make her excuses to Mrs Pettigrew and perhaps persuade Pete to do the search instead. After all, the woman was dead. Finding out how or why wouldn't change things.

"Are you seriously going to lie there instead of helping me?" Indignation sharpened the ghost's voice, climbing into registers it should stay away from in fear of being called shrill.

"You can give it a go yourself if you want to find out so desperately," Emily replied, not even cracking an eyelid. "Perhaps you'll surprise yourself and be a poltergeist."

The frustrated gasps and cries soon belied that expectation, but Emily dropped off to sleep despite the noise. One positive note for overtaxing her body during the day. She must remember the trick for the next time insomnia came calling.

An exasperated curse was the last thing Emily heard before she fell sound asleep.

CHAPTER FIVE

"*Y*ou don't need to explain," Pete said as Emily started on her well-rehearsed speech for why she needed to look up Mrs Pettigrew's death notice. "I've done the same before when I grew curious. As long as you're just reading publicly available information, there's no harm in it. I'll be glad to help."

She closed her eyes in relief. She could now shove her worst fear back into the depths of her stomach where it belonged. "Thank you."

"It's no trouble. I know well enough how difficult it is to not be able to do everything you want, anymore. If I can help, I'll always be glad too."

"Why do you need help?" Mrs Pettigrew drifted back from a thorough examination of the books on offer. "Surely, you're not so old you don't know how to Google something?"

Emily ignored the ghost, the same as she had all morning. Whether death had sharpened her tongue, or this was the personality Mrs Pettigrew had always been afflicted with, she neither knew nor cared.

Keeping the barbs from striking her was all that concerned Emily.

"Here it goes." Pete turned the laptop screen towards her, then smacked his forehead as he remembered. "Just a second. There's a read-aloud setting if you give me a moment. I'll set it up with speech input, too, then you can use it with voice commands."

"Are you illiterate?" The ghost peered over Emily's shoulder as Pete scrolled through the settings pane. "Have I wound up with someone who's a bit of a thicky?"

Although her hands closed into tight fists, Emily stopped herself from responding. The ghost didn't deserve the courtesy of an answer, and she didn't need her new co-worker thinking she was mad.

"I think this is it." Pete's tongue pressed up into the gap in his front teeth as he clicked on a command.

A robotic voice read out the heading on the page.

"Thank you," Emily said in relief, pulling the laptop closer as Pete walked off to greet a customer.

Pete had left the cursor at a point too far up the page and listed off the grieving family members for an Elizabeth Maidshead. After finishing the legion of relatives, the voice moved to the notice for Mrs Pettigrew.

"Cynthia," Emily exclaimed as the computer recited the passage. "It suits you."

"That's why I selected it," the ghost agreed with a satisfied purr. "You'd never believe the monstrosity of a name my mother saddled me with."

Remembering that curiosity killed the cat, Emily refrained from asking. She frowned as the digital voice read out the words, "Died peacefully at home."

"That can't be right."

Cynthia frowned and bent to peer at the screen. "It

doesn't sound right to me, either," she said, straightening up again. "What possible reason would my spirit have to hang around if I died of natural causes?"

"I don't know."

Pete turned his head toward her and Emily dropped her voice. "Perhaps we can visit your house again and learn more. I'm sure your stepson had a different view on how you died."

"Gregory?" The ghost raised her right eyebrow. "When did you ever talk to him? That boy only leaves his room to grab snacks."

Wary of drawing any more attention from Pete, Emily made the trek upstairs, her stiff limbs nagging at her the whole way. With the door closed against eavesdroppers, she stared at Mrs Pettigrew. The woman had floated upstairs with such ease she felt a deep stab of envy.

With a shake of her head, Emily dismissed the emotion. "I talked to Gregory while he was helping me take the boxes to the car."

"I suppose he's happy to see the back of me," the ghost said in a voice dripping with self-pity.

Emily could certainly sympathise with anyone taking that view.

"He put a brave face on it, but it was clear to me he genuinely missed you. I think your death hit him hard."

The glorious smile that resulted from those words made Emily sorry she'd said anything.

"What did he say about how I died?"

Emily shook her head. "It doesn't matter. I'm sure if we ask him again, we'll soon find out the truth." She paused and bit her lip. "I wonder if taking you back to your home will help you find your way to the next..."

She trailed off, unsure what words to use, and ended up just flapping her hand instead.

"I think the concept you're reaching for is heaven," Mrs Pettigrew said with a sniff. "Or do you think so badly of me?"

"I've never given it much consideration before," Emily lied. For many months as her injured body healed in a hospital bed, she'd filled her mind with thoughts of what might wait as an alternative. Each of them had sounded better than the constant pain she'd lived with at the time.

"Spirit realm." The ghost tipped her head to one side, listening to how it sounded. "How about we call it that?"

Emily nodded. "It sounds fine. If your house doesn't bring any suggestions of what to do, we can try the grave-yard next. It seems to work in movies."

"Great idea. Let's go," Mrs Pettigrew said, drifting halfway through the door.

When Emily didn't follow, the ghost paused and looked back with a frown.

"I can't go now," Emily explained, subduing the satisfied expression that wanted to spread itself across her face. "I've got a full day's work in front of me. If you don't want to stay here, float off somewhere else and occupy yourself for a while."

"Doing what? I can't touch anything or eat or drink. The entire world might as well be off limits."

"Look at something pretty. There're lovely gardens around the town, or you could go down to the homestead cottage and read all about the first settlers."

"Been there. Done that. I've been at a loose end in this town many a time before."

"Then sit in the corner and be quiet," Emily said in a stern voice. "It's only my second day on the job and I can't afford to lose it because some dead woman's distracting me."

With a scornful expression, Mrs Pettigrew settled into a corner of the room, staring from the dormer window at the pedestrians wandering along the street, each of them with a place to go.

THEY SET off to Mrs Pettigrew's after Emily finished work for the day. During her hours at the charity shop, she'd been excited to unearth a cream Crown Lynn Swan, medium sized.

Supposedly a vase, she didn't think anyone had ever successfully used it in that way. The post-war restrictions in place during the era they were first crafted had demanded goods have a purpose, instead of existing only for decoration.

A large hollow in the middle of the gracious curves might theoretically fit the bill, but any florist attempting to insert a bouquet would soon find the blooms poking out at very odd angles.

The large and the small sculptures of the swan were common enough to find with a good rummage through a multitude of garage sales on a Saturday morning, but far fewer of the medium vases had ever been sold. It gave Emily a warm glow to know a lucky collector could soon complete their set.

"I feel nothing," Mrs Pettigrew said after a few minutes spent staring up at her house. "Should I go inside, do you think?"

"I'm not sure. I don't really want anyone to see me again. Not after taking up so much of their time yesterday."

Emily shifted her weight from one foot to the other. Each leg hurt with the same dull ache, as though she had a tooth cavity in her hip bones.

A curtain twitched in an upstairs window and she stepped back, feeling her cheeks flood with colour. Even though she was just standing outdoors on the footpath, she felt like a trespasser with no right to be anywhere near the house.

"Oh, look." Mrs Pettigrew ran a few steps along the berm, waving to the gardener.

"He won't be able to see you," Emily said with a laugh, then clapped a hand over her mouth. *Or hear you, so it'll look as though I'm talking to myself!*

Cynthia continued to stare as the man trimmed back the camelia bushes along the side of the house. They were tall, reaching far past the spouting. For such slow-growing plants, it betrayed their age.

As Emily stared at the ghost with a concerned glance on her face, Mrs Pettigrew twisted a strand of hair around her finger and chewed on the corner of her lip. When the gardener glanced toward the footpath, she rose on the balls of her feet and clasped her hands behind her waist.

With a jolt, Emily realised the woman was flirting. Even though the poor man couldn't see her.

Turning with an amused smile on her lips, she saw the gardener striding straight towards them. Too late to run away or duck behind the shelter of a neighbour's fence.

You've been caught!

"Hey, there," the gardener said in his slow voice. "Did you forget something yesterday?"

Emily shook her head, confusion turning her mute. As he continued to stare, the gardener reminded her of an old-style movie star. Give him a shave and he could do a passable Cary Grant impression. No wonder Mrs Pettigrew was so smitten.

"I'm sorry," Emily said as she regained her voice. "I didn't come here to do anything but have another look. The house is so lovely, and I was rushing around yesterday so I didn't have time to take in more than a few glances."

He nodded as though the feeble excuse was reasonable. "Yeah, it's a nice place."

"Especially the garden," Mrs Pettigrew burst out. "Abraham's more than welcome to trim my topiary, any day."

Emily blushed and closed her eyes. "I didn't catch your name, yesterday," she said.

"Abraham Greening," he said with a slow smile. "You can tell I was born to be a gardener with a surname like that."

The ghost burst out with a coquettish giggle and Emily gave a tongue-tied nod. "Well"—she clapped her hands together—"don't let me keep you from your work. I'll be on my way."

"You should come inside for a cup of tea," the man said, jerking his head back towards the house. "I'm about due for a break. If we catch Hilda in a good mood, she'll make you a hot chocolate to die for. Might even give you a proper tour of the place."

"Oh, I couldn't put you two out like that," Emily said, shaking her head.

"It's no inconvenience. Between you and me, she loves to show the place off." Abraham glanced over his shoulder, then bent forward and whispered, "I think Hilda likes to pretend the place is hers. Especially now the missus isn't around."

"Peanut!"

Emily stepped back in surprise, her gaze jerked from Abraham's piercing blue-eyed stare to Mrs Pettigrew. A grey oriental cat, whitening belly placing in it the bracket of old-age, came running up and wound itself around and between the ghost's legs. As Emily watched, she patted the purring feline, the cat arching its back at the stroke.

"He can feel me," the ghost said, turning wide eyes towards Emily. "Will you look at that!"

"What's up with you, old fellow?" Abraham said, squatting and clicking his fingers until the cat came running. "You've been sitting in the hot sun for too long again, eh?"

"Come back here, Peanut." Mrs Pettigrew clapped her hands against the top of her thighs. "Come to Mummy."

Although she tried again to regain the animal's attention, Abraham lifted him up and tucked the cat under his arm. "Well, if you're sure you won't come inside...?"

Emily nodded. "I'm sure, but thanks very much for the offer."

"I'll see you around town I suppose." Abraham gave a curt nod and walked off, clicking his tongue to soothe Peanut.

A neighbour stared at Emily over the fence. It made her so uncomfortable she went back to the car. When Mrs Pettigrew joined her, it was with a glum expression on her face.

"All that did was make me miss Peanut. He's been with me every day since my marriage. I don't suppose you'd be willing to go back tonight and steal him?"

"You suppose right," Emily said, pointing the car toward the graveyard. "And I've got my fingers crossed it's because you'll be long gone by then."

"You know how to make a girl feel welcome," Mrs Pettigrew snapped, then fell into blessed silence.

The graveyard sat a few minutes' drive out of the town

centre. Emily supposed at the time of construction it had been far enough away to not scare the residents at night.

Now, leafy green suburbs stuffed full of young couples with children had sprung up around it. Given the growth in Pinetar township since she'd been a youngster, it was likely they'd soon move it elsewhere.

"I used to like coming here," Mrs Pettigrew said, walking through the wrought-iron gates. "I'd make gravestone rubbings of the old markers to work out what they said."

Emily hooked up an eyebrow at that but said nothing. She preferred it when her unwanted guest kept quiet so didn't want to encourage conversation.

"This is it." They walked into a newer part of the cemetery. The graves here were a mix of bare plots or fresh headstones. Off to the side, the children's cemetery was a riot of colour and plastic shapes, but in the adult section, things were far more subdued.

"A plaque," Mrs Pettigrew said with a moue of distaste. "Is that all Nathaniel thought I was worth?"

"The headstone will come later if he's ordered one," Emily explained. In her earlier job, she'd worked through budget advice with families beset by tragedy often enough to know the exorbitant cost of burying a loved one.

"They don't have them lying around at the ready. The marble is cut to order, and the engraving is hard work. It has to be tough stone. Otherwise, the words would fade away in a few years. That means cutting it with a diamond-headed tip and there's a waiting list."

"You're a bit gruesome, did you know?" Mrs Pettigrew shook her head and looked out over the immaculate grounds. "Perhaps your macabre interests are why you can see ghosts?"

"I can't see ghosts, I can see you. Believe me, if I thought it would stop, I'd give up all my hobbies and interests at once." Emily rubbed her fingers along the length of her scar, then sighed, regretting the harsh words. "Besides, I know this stuff because of work, not because I'm interested."

She turned back to Mrs Pettigrew to see what effect her words had, then twisted in a complete circle, staring around the cemetery.

The ghost was gone. It was as if her grave had swallowed her up while Emily looked the other way. She hesitated by the graveside, unsure if she should pursue the missing woman. After a short tussle, she decided not to and felt instantly relieved.

If someone had asked her to imagine a ghost, she'd never in a million years have created someone so sharp-tongued and selfish.

She slid her foot along the plaque, brushing away a few stray tendrils of grass with her toe. The cemetery groundskeeper must have mown the lawn recently as the loose blades hadn't yet turned brown.

The entire place was peaceful, so long as her mind didn't dwell on the multitude of dead bodies buried close around her. Emily was tempted to sit on a nearby bench and think through her day.

But, if she did that, the muscles in her legs would tighten and she'd struggle with the return walk to the car. With a sigh, Emily turned from the grave and struggled along the uneven lawn to the concrete path.

If she died, would her brother inter her in a place as nice as this one? Or would he leave it in the hands of the council and her lawyers, letting strangers sort out her remains as they'd sort out her estate?

She and Harvey had never shared the close bond Emily

admired and envied in other siblings. As soon as they were out of their parents' house, they each headed their own way, intent on fulfilling their ambitions without the intrusion of relatives in their lives.

Still, he'd made contact with her when the hospital tracked him down as her next of kin. It was Emily who'd then let the renewed relationship lapse, leaving it until tomorrow, then the day after, to get back to him until getting in touch made no sense at all.

Her car provided a welcome rest area for Emily to sit and think. She laid her head and arms on the steering wheel, letting old memories and new filter into her mind until she grew sleepy. Tears of exhaustion and self-pity flowed down the side of her face.

"Stop crying, Scarface, I'm back." Mrs Pettigrew appeared in the passenger side seat like a developing Polaroid image. A snapshot of disaster.

Emily wiped at her cheeks, sniffing, and pulled a handkerchief out of her sleeve. "Where did you get to?"

"I just slipped away for a few minutes. Watching you stumble from side to side like Frankenstein's monster was getting on my nerves." The ghost tittered to herself, staring out the side window. "That's fitting, isn't it? After all, you look like you're stitched together from different people."

The tears returned with a vengeance. Emily couldn't stop them from pouring forth, even though she felt rage inside her, not sorrow.

"How dare you speak to me like that? Get out of my car at once!"

Mrs Pettigrew stared at her as though she were crazy. "But you're the only one who can see me. Where else am I meant to go?"

Emily's mouth dropped open. Fury lit up her chest with

the hot burn of an infection, but she couldn't give voice to the thoughts flaming in her mind.

The ghost held up a hand. "Anyway, stop whatever you're doing. I've remembered something important. I was thinking of Gregory and how he used to trail around behind me when I first married Nathaniel, chattering away non-stop. Whenever my hand was free, he'd insert his sticky fingers into mine and squeeze tight."

"Lovely." The muscles in Emily's face drooped until it became as deadpan as her voice. "I'm so glad you came back to tell me that."

"No, no! Listen! I thought of him as a child, then another memory of Gregory flashed up. I saw him standing over me and this time his hands were sticky with blood. My blood."

Emily shook her head, the emotions whirling inside preventing her from following the conversation. "And?"

"And I didn't die peacefully at home, that's a load of rubbish. I was murdered!"

CHAPTER SIX

"*M*urdered?" Emily tried to keep the shock out of her voice. The why seemed obvious to her, even on short acquaintance, but she asked the other question, "Who by?"

Mrs Pettigrew flapped her hands again. "I don't know that bit. Somebody in the household, I guess. Probably Gregory since he was the one covered in my blood."

"You think your stepson attacked you?" Emily pulled at the front of her blouse, twiddling a pearl button. "I suppose we'd better report this crime to the police."

The ghost sat back in her seat, huffing out a sigh. "You believe me?"

"Of course, I do." Emily started the car and shot a glance of curiosity over to her companion. "You're the only person who would know for sure. Why wouldn't I trust you?"

"No reason at all."

Mrs Pettigrew suddenly sat forward and grabbed at Emily's arm, the fingertips disappearing until she jerked her hand back. "I wonder if this is the thing keeping me here. If we find the killer and solve the crime, perhaps I'll move on to a better place."

Emily bit her lip against the words that wanted to come —*or a worse one*. She needed to keep these dreadful thoughts from popping up inside her head. Had they been this terrible before the accident or was it the bang on the head that had turned her into a grouch?

"I hope the police don't make me come with them when they go to arrest Gregory." It would be terrible to stand and point the finger, condemning someone she didn't know to life in prison. "Although, I guess they don't usually invite a witness along for the ride."

"No, they don't. And you're not a witness."

"I am to you. Since I'm the only person who can see you in this form, I think it counts. I'm your locum eyewitness."

From the corner of her vision, Emily saw the ghost roll her eyes, but she clamped her lips into a firm line and concentrated on the road ahead of her. No matter what the haughty ghost next to her thought, Emily would play an important role in seeing justice done.

For the first time in a long while, she felt useful. No, not just that. Necessary. Vital.

"What are you smiling about? I tell you I've been murdered, and you've been grinning ever since."

"I'm just thinking how nice it'll be to sleep in my bed tonight without you staring at me."

Emily pulled into the police depot carpark and chose a spot. With nothing but the police vehicles there, she was spoiled.

"What are you doing?" she asked as Mrs Pettigrew strode toward the station. Emily heaved herself out of the car, locking the door behind her out of habit, though it must be the safest place to park in town. "I'll go in by myself."

"But…" The ghost's face twisted. "I have to explain everything to the officers."

"I'm doing that. You stay in the car unless I come calling for you. Or wait outside and look in through the window if that suits better." Emily crossed her arms when Mrs Pettigrew's lip pooched out. "Don't sulk. I can hardly concentrate on telling the police everything if you're hanging around, chatting in my ear. They'll think I'm mad."

"Make sure you explain it carefully, then." Mrs Pettigrew sat on the bench outside the entrance. "I don't want my chance at justice to go down the pan just because you don't know how to talk to people."

A retort almost slipped out of Emily's mouth, but she clamped her lips shut. Standing outside the station, arguing with somebody no one else could see, wouldn't make a good first impression.

"I'll try my hardest," she said instead since that was the truth. "And I'll try not to be too long."

The door to the station had a large handle and when Emily put her hand on it, all the doubts in the world beset her. *What was she doing? The men inside wouldn't believe she could see ghosts! By telling them the truth she'd probably wind up locked in a room at the psychiatric hospital for the night.*

She flicked a glance at Mrs Pettigrew. On the other hand, if she didn't tell the police the truth and get rid of the ghost, she might well end up in the same place.

With a deep breath, Emily pulled on the handle and walked into the air-conditioned lobby. She walked straight up to the counter before her courage could abandon her and placed both hands palm-down on the varnished wood.

The officer who walked over to her was young, in his mid-twenties, maybe.

"I need to report a murder," Emily said and watched as his eyes opened wide. "My friend Cynthia Pettigrew was killed a few weeks ago. Her stepson Gregory Pettigrew is the murderer."

AN HOUR LATER, Emily bitterly regretted her impulsive decision. She should have waited until she had something more to go on than the word of a rich ghost.

At least she'd caused a great amount of jollity to be had by the officers on duty. After being taken into an interview room to explain the details of her case, the first officer, PC Perry, couldn't wait to open the door and called out to his friend. "Hey, Mitchell. I think the lady in here is friends with your favourite tipster, Crystal."

While Emily frowned, not understanding the reference, the second officer scanned her from head to toe, shaking his head dismissively. "You're part of the psychic brigade too, love?"

"I'm nobody's love," Emily said through a throat that had tightened to the thinness of a straw. She walked out of the room. "I'm here to report a serious crime."

"Go on," Officer Perry urged her. "Tell PC Mitchell how you know the details of the murder."

"I've been haunted by the ghost of Cynthia Pettigrew. She told me who murdered her a few minutes ago, and I rushed here at once."

When the two men burst into outright laughter, Emily stamped her foot. A movement her hip made her immediately regret. That wasn't the only thing she was regretting by then, of course.

"Stop laughing. This is serious." She banged her fists on

a nearby desk and stared at the men from under a frown so deep, everything appeared shadowed. "I'm reporting a murder and it's your duty to investigate it."

"I thought we didn't need to," the first officer said, trying to hold his expression in a neutral position. "From what you said, we just need to take this ghost's word for it and get down to the house to arrest the man right away."

"That would be ideal," Emily said with a gasp of relief. "If Gregory is left alone, thinking he got away with this dreadful crime, then there's no telling what he'll do next."

She realised her mistake again as the two men once more exploded into renewed laughter. Their giggling sounded like the hyenas on the wildlife shows on television. Either that or the piercing cry of the human teenage girl.

"Who is your superior officer?" Emily demanded, snapping her fingers to gain PC Perry's attention. "I want to speak to your sergeant at once!"

"I wouldn't recommend that. Sergeant Winchester is less likely to take your report in as good a spirit as we have." Perry tilted his head to one side. "It's a crime to waste police time, you know. If you want to escalate this ridiculous accusation, you could be facing jail time or a hefty fine."

"There's nothing ridiculous about my accusation." Emily felt tears of anger and shame prick at the corners of her eyes and shook her head to drive them away. "Murder is the worst thing that can be done to a person. No matter how I came by the information, you shouldn't dismiss it. The man might kill again."

An office door at the back of the large reception space suddenly opened. A heavy-set man with a glower on his face peered out. "What's going on out here? Why're you all making such a racket?"

"Sorry, Sarge," PC Perry said, giving a stiff bow. "We're

dealing with a strange complaint, but I think we're almost sorted."

"No, you're not. Neither of you is listening to me, you're too busy having a laugh." Emily moved around the side of the cubicle to get a better look. "I'm here to report a murder and both of your officers here have acted disgracefully."

"She's a nutter, Sarge," PC Mitchell hurried to say. "Friend of Crystal's."

"I don't know anyone called Crystal. Why do you keep saying that?"

"There's no need to raise your voice." The sergeant skewered Emily with a steely stare. "Who's been murdered?"

When PC Perry opened his mouth to answer on Emily's behalf, the sergeant flicked a hand at him to silence the response. "I want to hear it from the lady."

Although her legs were now shaking, Emily straightened her spine and looked the man straight in the eye. "Cynthia Pettigrew was murdered. Her stepson Gregory is the killer."

The man didn't respond for a second except to pull his bushy salt and pepper eyebrows together in thought. "The coroner ruled that one accidental death."

"Well, it wasn't." Emily wrung her hands together, the palms sweaty. "It was a murder."

"Come through here." The sergeant disappeared into his office, leaving Emily to follow him into the room.

Her stomach took a joy ride, rising up and twisting before plummeting back into place. The inside of the office was a mess of whiteboards, filing cabinets, and paper. Open case files sat on top of his desk, a situation he soon remedied while waving Emily into a chair.

"Sorry about those lads out there. This is a hard job and

we see a lot of the worst of people, so they take their fun where they can get it." He sat heavily in a swivel chair that groaned under the weight. "It can be harsh on the receiving end."

"I came here to report a serious crime, not to be made fun of."

The man nodded and pulled at a drawer, an effort that took a few goes. The cabinet made a horrible squealing noise of wood on wood before it opened. He flicked through the suspended files hanging there, giving a satisfied grunt as he pulled one out. "Here we go. Mrs Cynthia Jane Pettigrew nee Morland. Cause of death, an accident."

Emily leaned forward, peering at the mess of lines and drawings. "Can I see that?" she asked as if the words would make sense to her. Perhaps she should have let the ghost come inside and let her read over the sergeant's shoulder.

Not that it mattered. The man shook his head and snapped the manila folder closed before shoving it back into the overcrowded drawer. It took him the same effort to close it as it had to wrench it open. "No, you can't. It's an official file."

"Just because the coroner made a ruling doesn't mean it's the truth." Emily gave a sharp nod. "He'll just need to reopen it, while you investigate my concerns."

"Except you haven't told me your concerns. You've made an accusation." The sergeant clasped his hands together and peered intently at Emily. "Do you have any evidence of this crime?"

She opened her mouth, and he held up one hand.

"Apart from the word of a ghost?"

Emily snapped her mouth shut again, a slow heat building in her cheeks. "No. I don't have evidence."

As a satisfied expression crossed the sergeant's face, she

snapped, "I thought that was your job. Aren't you even going to try to investigate this matter?"

"We have, and so has the coroner. We're both satisfied there's nothing suspicious about this death and the case is closed. To reopen it, we'll need a lot more than just the word of someone who believes she can talk to ghosts."

"I'd like to see the coroner's report," Emily said, folding her arms across her chest. "I think it's the least you can do."

"No, the least I can do is what I'm about to, which is nothing. If you want to get hold of that report, fill out an official information act request and forward it to the office."

Emily's mouth set in a determined line. Yes, she'd do that. She'd get the report and prove these laughing fools wrong.

Except you can't even read the report, let alone fill it out.

"Would you be able to help me with that?" Emily asked in a small voice. Her fingers reached up to trace the line of her scar. "I had an accident. It interferes with some tasks."

The sergeant looked at her with pity. He scrawled something on a note and Emily felt a sense of despair. She clenched her hands together hard and tried to think how to say the same thing again without losing every last scrap of her dignity.

"Take this to the library tomorrow." The sergeant held out the note to her, smiling when she took it. "The librarian will be able to take you through the whole process, including filling out the form for you. She's used to it."

The tears from earlier were back. Emily sniffed them back and stood up, nodding to the sergeant. "Thank you. I'll be back later with more information."

"Not information. Evidence."

She nodded again. "Okay. Evidence."

CHAPTER SEVEN

"Well, that was embarrassing," Mrs Pettigrew said by way of greeting as Emily walked out of the station. "I could tell from the view through the window you made the wrong impression."

Emily's temper exploded. "I didn't give them the wrong impression. It was you who did that. Until I mentioned the intensely irritating ghost who won't leave me alone, they were taking me seriously. You're the one who caused all the amusement. Now, they couldn't care less if you were murdered and neither could I!"

She slammed her car door, the action giving her so much satisfaction Emily wished she could open it up and do it again. Nothing stopped her, so she did.

"Quiet! Those officers will hear you making all this noise and come out to see what's happening, then you'll look even more of a fool."

"Worse than a woman who believes she can talk to ghosts?" Emily tried to jam the key into the ignition and seethed when it skittered all the way around instead. "You're probably not even there. You're probably just a figment of my imagination who thinks I deserve to be punished even more than I have been."

She stopped short, eyes widening as she stared out the windscreen. "Am I already dead? Is that it? I'm in hell and this is the diabolical punishment Satan is inflicting on me for a life lived in sin."

"Don't be foolish. You're just as alive as I—"

Mrs Pettigrew cut herself off, folding her arms and staring out the passenger side window.

Emily snorted in amusement. "You were saying?"

"How about you drive us home for the night and we can pick up this confusing conversation in the morning?"

"No. I want to go back to work. There's a heap of boxes there with a multitude of stuff from your life inside. If you're real and you genuinely were murdered, we should start there."

Mrs Pettigrew didn't offer a better suggestion, so Emily drove the short distance to the charity shop. During the day, its large downstairs windows appeared open and welcoming. In the gloom of night, they were eyes, cavernous and hungry.

Emily hunched her shoulders as she walked inside the shop. She didn't know if being here after hours broke the terms of her employment, but she knew Pete wouldn't like it. She navigated in stumbling steps using only the lights from the streetlamps outside the store.

"Boo!" Mrs Pettigrew yelled as Emily opened the upstairs door. For a second, she held a hand up to her racing heart, sure it was about to explode. When it settled, she wished the ghost had solidity, so she could give her a satisfying thump.

"Won't someone see the light up here?" Mrs Pettigrew

asked as Emily turned on the light and she gave a shrug in response.

"Perhaps. But I need to be able to see and I don't have a torch on me. How about you?"

"Oh, yes. I have torches stashed everywhere."

"I meant about seeing in the dark, you nincompoop."

"No. Being dead hasn't granted me any superpowers I know of."

"Except extreme annoyance."

Emily mumbled that last under her breath, but Mrs Pettigrew heard. "In truth, I was far more irritating when I was alive. That and looking beautiful were my only skills."

"Pity you can't help me with these boxes," Emily exclaimed as she manhandled one onto the floor. "Why does everything you owned weigh an absolute tonne?"

Instead of responding, Mrs Pettigrew gave a strangled cry. Emily stood up, taking a step towards her before she realised the ghost was staring straight at her own portrait.

"That seems to be a common reaction to the painting," Emily said with a chuckle. "When Gregory saw it in the passenger seat, he screamed so loudly I nearly died of a heart attack on the spot."

"Why were you driving around with my portrait in the car?" Mrs Pettigrew asked in an annoyed tone. "In fact, what are you doing with this at all? Nathaniel commissioned this for my thirtieth birthday. It should be hanging in his study or the grand hall."

"It turned up in the first box." Emily lowered herself to her knees. "I guess the household couldn't wait to get rid of it."

She winced as the words came out of her mouth. Even for a snippy conversation that was one step too far. When she turned to Mrs Pettigrew to apologise, tears glistened in the ghost's eyes.

"I said I was annoying. Perhaps I hadn't understood until now, they actually hated me."

"I'm sure that's wrong." Emily sat back on her heels. "Gregory made a show of disdain, but it didn't last long. He really misses you. Hilda was a tougher nut to crack but even she appeared to think of you with some fondness."

"Probably thinking of how glad she was I'm dead," Miss Pettigrew snapped, back to her usual self. "Where's the frame gone? Have you sold that already?"

"No." Emily shuffled over to the painting on her hands and knees. "It came with the replacement frame already on it, although I could see at once it wasn't the original."

"They kept the frame and tossed away the painting." Mrs Pettigrew's voice was so low Emily had to strain to hear her.

"I originally assumed the owner sold it when they were on hard times. I suppose that's not likely though, is it? Were you and Nathaniel hard up?"

"Not enough to sell off a five-thousand-dollar frame. I thought it was a downgrade to settle for only two million because of the prenuptial agreement."

"You were getting a divorce?" Emily frowned at the news. "I guess it explains why so many of your possessions ended up here."

"I guess." The ghost sighed and floated over to the dormer window. "It'll sound stupid, but I still thought Nathaniel loved me. When I asked for a divorce, it was really to get something I wanted that he refused to pay for. Instead of giving in, he agreed to end the marriage so quickly I was insulted."

Emily thought of a boy she'd broken up with at University. When she'd decided to stay on in Christchurch for a job rather than travel overseas as they'd planned, instead of the tears she'd expected, he'd grinned. "That's rough."

"For all the problems money is meant to solve, it doesn't do a good job at making anyone happy."

"I guess it's just an easier goal for most people to focus on than actually mending what's wrong with their life."

"Who'd even buy an empty frame?"

Emily gave up any pretence of sorting through the boxes and stared at the portrait. "It's a common size for a painting. I guess, if it was expensive, someone might snap it up as a bargain."

"It was gold-plating over hand-cast metal. Compared to this tacky wooden thing, it was gorgeous."

"How about I open all the boxes and you see if there's anything immediately jumps out at you as suspicious?" Emily moved back to the open one, fearful that if they sat and considered the portrait any longer, they'd never get anything else done.

"I can do that. Although, I don't know what something suspicious would look like."

"Anything out of place, I guess." Emily grinned. "Or bloodstains on a baseball bat, that sort of thing."

WHEN THE ALARM blared the next morning, Emily groaned and cracked open an eye. She could have sworn she'd only just laid down on the bed, but here it was—bright morning.

They'd stayed at the charity shop until close on midnight the evening before, but they might as well have not bothered. Nothing in the boxes brought back any memories. At least, not connected to the murder. From the array of hurt expressions that crossed Mrs Pettigrew's face during the night, they contained a boatload of pain.

"About time," the ghost grumped as her way of saying good morning. "It's so boring here with nobody around to talk to."

For Emily's part, the ghost appeared to talk *at* her rather than *to* her, but it was far too soon in the day to start complaining. She yawned and pulled her laptop towards her, starting up the button Pete had set up to enable voice commands.

"Medium, Pinetar Township," she said aloud, talking into the screen because she was unsure where the microphone was. Wherever the device was located, it heard her well enough. A circle of dots lit up the monitor and a browser tab opened.

"Crystal Dreaming," Mrs Pettigrew read aloud over her shoulder with a snort. "I hope that name is made up. Imagine going to school with kids teasing you about that clanger every day."

"Does it have a phone number?" Emily asked.

"You're not actually going to call this woman, are you?" When Emily nodded, the ghost rolled her eyes. "She's as fake as the days are long."

"Or she has a gift and she might be able to help us both out."

Mrs Pettigrew rolled her eyes again. "Whatever."

Emily pulled out her phone and following Mrs Pettigrew's instruction, hit the buttons until it connected and began ringing. Soon enough, the call went to voicemail.

"I'd like to make an appointment for a reading," Emily said after the beep. "I work during the day, but I'm available at midday for an hour or after work from five onwards."

She rang off, feeling silly. Now her consciousness was more fully engaged, the idea didn't seem as brilliant as it had when she first woke.

"It should be good for a laugh," Mrs Pettigrew said, perhaps hoping to allay Emily's worries but managing to enforce them instead. "I wonder if Crystal uses a crystal ball." She hugged herself. "That would be too perfect."

"If she's the real deal, you can tell her all that yourself. I just hope she has some experience to help me. If she can wave a magic wand to get rid of you, it won't matter how much she charges."

"You know I'm standing right here." The ghost appeared upset. "If you want to talk about how awful I am, at least have the same courtesy as everyone else and do it behind my back."

"Sorry." Emily experienced genuine remorse. "I didn't get enough sleep and I'm taking it out on you. Plus, the reaction at the police station last night did nothing for my ego."

"I told you to take me in with you. I could've directed the conversation until they were all convinced."

"You can do that next time when we bring in the ton of evidence you're going to direct me to find."

Mrs Pettigrew tilted her head to one side, frowning. "What evidence?"

"The police need something solid before they'll look at your case again and I don't know what happened, so it'll have to come from you." Emily walked over and mimed rapping her knuckles near the ghost's head. "Get your thinking cap on."

"I've already thought about it. I've been doing nothing else. What about the coroner's report? When are you going to do that?"

Last night, Emily had thought she might be able to use

the voice commands on her computer to listen and fill out the form, but the document wasn't enabled to do that. She still had the scrap of paper with whatever reference the sergeant had jotted on it but the prospect of explaining her disability to yet another person didn't fill her with joy.

"If the medium doesn't call back to make an appointment, I'll use my lunch break today."

"Okay." Mrs Pettigrew looked thoughtful for a second. "If you do your work more quickly this morning, will Pete let you off earlier?"

"I don't really work *for* him, as such," Emily said, her brow creasing. "But if I don't get your boxes sorted ready to take to the auction house tomorrow, then I won't have any money coming in from sales this week. It'll take three weeks from now for the final sales to come through to the account. I can't postpone it any longer."

"Don't worry about that." The ghost looked even more satisfied with herself than usual. "You don't need to go through the box and guess the value for each item when I can stand there and tell you the exact provenance and worth of each object."

Emily glanced at her in surprise. "Do you seriously remember all of that?"

"They're my most treasured possessions in the world," Mrs Pettigrew said with a catch in her voice. "Bet your bottom dollar, I remember."

CHAPTER EIGHT

The medium hadn't called back before lunchtime, so when the clock struck one o'clock and Pete came back from his break, Emily made a beeline for the library. Without an idea of how long the process would take, she munched a sandwich while walking along the street.

"If you want to keep trim as you get older," Mrs Pettigrew said, "you should try to cut out carbs."

Emily looked at her six-grain sandwich bread, brown and tough, much like the leathery skin on the back of her hands. She remembered the bread from her childhood, springy, thick-crusted, and any variety you could imagine so long as it was white.

Nowadays, she felt the same pang of guilt grabbing hold of a loaf of white toast bread as she did buying a bag of lollies.

"I've given up enough stuff lately, thank you," she said and popped the last bite into her mouth. She tossed the screwed-up plastic wrap went into a roadside rubbish bin.

"The least you can do is add a few raw vegetables."

Sergeant Winchester's comment from the night before

popped up in Emily's mind and she smiled. "No, the least I can do is nothing, so I'll choose that."

They sauntered the last few metres to the library. "Remember, I don't want you talking in here. I get enough strange looks out on the street where it's possible I could be having a Bluetooth conversation on my phone. Indoors, it won't work at all."

Mrs Pettigrew gazed into the far distance as though Emily must be talking to someone else. Perhaps a phantom child.

With one last stern glance of warning, Emily pulled open the doorway to the library, revelling in the chill of the first gust of air-conditioning after the heat of the sun outdoors. In a far cry from the dim libraries she remembered from university, the building sported large windows and a high ceiling, filling the space with light.

Her bank of memories was becoming outdated. Time had turned even this familiar township into a foreign world.

A row of tables in the middle of the room held a bank of computers and Emily made a beeline for them, then looked around for help. A smiling young woman engaged in a conversation nearby gave her a nod, and finished her conversation, sending the other midday patron on their way to the large stacks on the left-hand-side wall.

"I wanted to submit an official information request," Emily said, pulling the card the sergeant had given her out of her pocket. "I spoke to a policeman yesterday who said I could get help with that here."

"Of course," the young librarian said with a smile, a frown briefly caressing her forehead as she read the card. "Take a seat here, and I'll log in. It's been a wee while since I've filled one out, so apologies if it takes some time."

"I'm in no hurry," Emily said, flushing with gratitude

that the woman was helping without needing a long-winded explanation. She sat in the chair and watched as the woman's hands went to work, sailing gracefully over the keys.

Even in her old job, Emily had never learned to touch-type. Apart from the numerical keyboard on the side. She'd been able to work that blindfolded for the length of a spreadsheet screen.

"Cynthia Pettigrew," the librarian repeated when Emily gave her the name to enter. Her eyebrows rose, and her mouth pursed for the second, then fell back into its earlier smile as she typed in the information.

"Did you know her?"

The ghost was already shaking her head, a moue of distaste on her lips.

"No, apart from knowing who she was." The librarian shrugged. "In a town this small, it's hard not to know everyone by name after a while, whether you've been introduced or not."

Emily laughed. "I'm still getting back to that point, but I know what you mean. When I was growing up here, I could walk into a room and tell you who was from town or outside in a glance."

"Even those who scrupulously keep their noses out of other people's business knew Cynthia Pettigrew," the librarian happily continued. "Not to speak ill of the dead, but that family had more than its share of troubles and I think a lot of them stemmed from her."

"What sort of troubles?" Emily kept her gaze fixed to the screen in a show of uninterest.

"The son, Gregory, got expelled from University for drugs," the woman confided in a whisper. "Not just taking them, either."

"He was selling them?" Emily gave a low whistle. "I wouldn't have thought they were in the income bracket for that sort of trouble."

"They're not as wealthy as it might appear," the librarian said, her smile turning to one of satisfaction. "Nathaniel Pettigrew's business interests have been sliding southward for quite some time. I've got a friend in the bank who says the house is mortgaged up to the hilt."

"What rubbish!" Mrs Pettigrew burst out. "I'm not the one getting my card declined at the supermarket, Miss know-it-all." She gave the librarian a prod with her finger and snarled when it produced no reaction.

Emily ignored her, concentrating on the screen and what the woman was saying. "It seems a bit strange," she commented in as deadpan a tone as possible. "They donated all the wife's belongings to the charity shop, and it's worth a great deal. If the family really were struggling, I'd expect them to sell it rather than donating it to a good cause."

The librarian shrugged again. "It'll be a tax write-off or something." She gave a quick glance around, then leaned in close again. "From what I heard, the Inland Revenue took a second look at the business's finances and decided to add a few zeros to the bill."

Again, Emily tried to keep her expression bland. If that were true, she should be able to verify it through the companies register. As long as the business was publicly listed, the finances should be disclosed.

Mrs Pettigrew cleared her throat loudly and Emily focused her attention back on the task in hand. "How long will it take for this application to go through?"

"The government rules stipulate the department has to provide an answer within three weeks," the librarian said, finishing off her typing and submitting the form. She signed out of the computer.

"That long?" Emily felt a rush of disappointment. She'd expected with the digital submission it would go much faster.

"And that's just to get an answer on whether you can have the information. There're no deadlines on the actual supply of the documents. Even if the coroner's office says yes, you're probably looking at a wait."

"Oh."

Emily's face must have fallen because the librarian touched a hand to her shoulder. "If it's important you get hold of it quicker than that, you could try asking the family. When the coroner entered his findings, he would've given a copy of the entire report to them."

Mrs Pettigrew shook her head.

"Thanks for helping me out," Emily said. "I owe you one."

"Don't be silly, that's what I'm here for," the librarian responded, her eyes scanning the room in search of another patron to aid. "You're welcome at any time."

The emergence back into the bright daylight had Emily blinking back tears. She stood in the doorway for a moment, letting her eyes adjust. The warmth and humidity outside were like an exhalation of a gigantic creature's fetid breath. A stock truck must be in the vicinity— the reek of lanolin and animal waste hung heavily in the air.

"Three weeks is far too long to wait," Mrs Pettigrew said with a sigh of disappointment. "I need to know all the facts now."

"Can you float into your house and have a search for it?"

The ghost snorted. "If Nathaniel has it lying open on

his desk, sure. If it's in his locked drawers or his filing cabinet..." She mimed the action, shaking her head.

"I suppose." Emily walked to a bench and sat, stretching out her leg. The right thigh muscle was twitching, and she kneaded it, trying to avoid a cramp. Just as she ready to stand, the mobile in her pocket buzzed. "Emily Curtis speaking."

"This is Crystal Dreaming. You left a message? I just wanted to get in touch and say I've got space free at five o'clock if you still want to meet today."

Emily nodded, giving Mrs Pettigrew a thumbs-up sign. "Fantastic."

THE FRONT LOUNGE of Crystal Dreaming's house served as her business. When Emily fought her way through the tangle of tinkling wind chimes and spinning dream catchers that lined the medium's porch, she hesitated before knocking.

"What's the problem?" Mrs Pettigrew said, folding her arms across her chest. "Having second thoughts?"

Yes. And third ones.

The policemen's cruel laughter from the evening before recurred to Emily. They'd mentioned Crystal then, a few times, using the same mocking tones. Did that mean she was about to meet with an ally or go sailing off the edge into pure madness?

Only one way to tell.

She rapped her knuckles on the door, too late seeing the neat button doorbell set next to the French sliders. A bustle of movement inside and the door slid open to show a plump and cheerful woman standing there.

Windswept. That was the first word that occurred to Emily. Crystal Dreaming looked like she'd just fought her way through a raging storm to reach the front door—her halo of curly brown hair, well-streaked with grey, stuck out in all directions above a comfortably large frame.

"Come in, you must be Emily," Crystal boomed, her voice as loud as the colourful pattern on her dress. "I've got the room all set up to go but if you need to take a few moments to get settled before we dig in, that's fine too."

The room had curtains half drawn to create an atmosphere of gloom. The windows being half-covered had done nothing to stop the heat of the day encroaching and the room felt stuffy. Emily reached up a hand to touch her own curls, drooping limply as they gave up the fight before it had begun.

"Take a seat here, love," Crystal said, pulling out a chair.

The heavy damask coating was embroidered to within an inch of its life with a pastoral scene. At a point in the past, it had split—maybe under the weight of an overburdened client—and the pink woollen stitching formed an incongruous scar.

"Oh, my goodness," Mrs Pettigrew exclaimed, then snickered. "She's actually got a crystal ball."

Since the large object sat pride of place in the centre of the table, Emily hardly needed her attention drawn to it. Crystal must have been reading her face because she reached out a hand to touch Emily on the arm.

"I can read cards or tea leaves if that's your preference. As long as the spirits are willing, I don't mind how they appear to me. I can intuit their message in whatever format makes you most comfortable."

"Can you interpret this?" Mrs Pettigrew shouted,

holding up a pair of fingers as rabbit's ears behind the medium's head.

Considering Crystal continued to beam out a beatific smile, Emily concluded she couldn't. Unless her relationship with the spirit world was very different to the one Emily had formed, she suspected they might be in the presence of a fraud.

Still, giving the woman the benefit of the doubt, Emily nodded. "The crystal ball is fine, I don't have another preference. I've never seen one before in real life. It's very pretty."

The ball did catch the dull light sneaking around the corners of the room and refracted it out into a roaring display of colour. Emily leaned forward, squinting and winking to see the difference it made.

"Steady on, there," Crystal said with a laugh. "I'm the one meant to stare into the ball and interpret its secrets. You can sit back and relax. I assure you, you're in safe hands."

"Safe from the ghost world, at least," Mrs Pettigrew said. She leaned onto the table on her elbows, sticking her face up close against the side of the globe. "See anything, lady? Catching a glimpse into the spirit realm, are you?"

Emily blinked her eyes, wishing she was alone so she could remonstrate with her ghostly guest. "Do you need me to tell you anything?"

"Not a thing, love. You can just sit back and relax." Crystal rearranged herself on her chair, dragging it closer and placing her hands either side of the ball. "If I have any trouble getting through, I might ask you to hold hands. We don't have to if you don't want, but it sometimes makes it easier to get in touch with the other side."

"Don't take her hands," Mrs Pettigrew said, standing back from the table. She wiped her palms against her ghost dress. "I think sweating is this woman's stock in trade, not communing with the dead."

The strain of ignoring her friend took a toll and the muscles in Emily's neck tightened.

"Don't look so worried, pet!" Crystal gave her a big wink. "Unless you've left a trail of dead bodies in your wake, there's nothing here to concern you."

Mrs Pettigrew laughed. "Apart from the fact you're being ripped off."

And maybe Crystal was listening in to the ghost's one-sided conversation, because she gave a start and sat back, drawing her hands into her lap. "I almost forgot to say. Payment is due up front. It'll be two hundred dollars for the first session and I give a discount if you book another one before you leave."

"That sounds very reasonable," Emily said, pulling her wallet out of her handbag. "Is cash okay?"

"Great." Crystal took the money out of her hand and counted it before tucking it into her bra. "If you need it in future, I've also got EFTPOS. I prefer debit cards, but I can process a credit card transaction for a slightly higher fee."

"I bet she can," the ghost said. Her eyes were glued to the medium's face with rapt attention. "She's a slick act, I'll give her that."

"Okay, love. Pop your hands flat on the table and relax. I'm going to reach out to whoever's here for you in the spirit world." Crystal tilted her head to one side. "Is there anyone specific you were hoping to connect with today? Your mum, for example."

Emily gave a small cry as memories crowded forward. How lovely would that be? To talk to her soft and loving mother instead of listening to the barbed tongue of Mrs Pettigrew for hours on end.

But she wasn't here for reminiscing. Work needed to be done.

She shook her head, lying through her teeth. "I've got nobody in mind. Just whoever's nearest. They don't need to be a relative of mine at all."

"Why don't you give her more pointers," Mrs Pettigrew growled. "Maybe toss my name into the ring while you're at it."

"Fine. Let me just close my eyes and get my bearings, then."

"Do I need to shut mine, too?"

"No, love. Not unless it makes you more comfortable."

Crystal Dreaming sat still for a moment, hands near to the globe as though it was a fire to warm them. The woman gave a low hum, under her breath. It sounded comforting. Emily found her mind wandering as the long minutes passed. The muggy heat in the room pulled her eyelids closed for longer with each blink.

"I can feel you, spirit. Do you wish to communicate with us today?"

Emily jerked upright, staring across the table at Mrs Pettigrew. When the ghost didn't say anything, she frowned and gave a sharp nod.

Mrs Pettigrew rolled her eyes but obliged. "I'm here and yes, I'd like to talk with you and Emily today."

The medium continued to keep her eyes closed in concentration. After another long pause, she asked, "Are you still there, spirit? Can you tell me your name?"

"It's Cynthia Pettigrew. I want to find out who murdered me."

Crystal opened her eyes. "Does the name Gary Hendermacht mean anything to you?"

A sick dread poured into Emily's stomach like an ice-cold liquid. She tried to shake her head, to say no. Instead, she gave a slow nod of recognition.

"Cynthia Pettigrew." The ghost waved her hands in front of Crystal. "Hello? Anybody there? I need to find a killer. Rather important."

"He's here in the room with me. Gary wants to tell you it wasn't your fault."

"Who the hell is Gary?" Mrs Pettigrew turned to Emily. "Do you know what she's talking about?"

"Gary is the person who caused my car accident," Emily explained. Her eyes stayed fixed on Crystal's, but she spoke for the benefit of the ghost. "He's very easy to look up on Google if you wanted to do that sort of thing. He broadsided my car and very nearly killed me. Certainly, he took away everything that meant something in my life."

She rose from the chair, hands and legs shaking so much Emily wasn't sure she could make it to the door. A tear escaped her eye, and she wiped it away with a vicious swipe of her hand.

"Perhaps he has something else to tell you," Crystal gushed. "Just sit back down and I'll—"

"I think we both know you're a fraud," Emily said. Her voice caught, and she had to steady herself on the back of the chair.

"What *is* this?" Crystal leapt to her feet, her expression turning from a polite smile into a glare. "Are you here to set me up? You don't think I know how these things go. Here"— she dug the cash out of her bosom and thrust it across the table—"take your money and get out of my house. This is my livelihood. I try to help people. You and your society just try to drag everyone—"

"What society?" Emily felt as flustered by the change of mood as she did by her anger. "I'm not with anyone and neither am I trying to bring you down. I came here because I stupidly thought you might have answers for me. There's a ghost standing a foot away from you who's driving me crazy and I hoped you'd be able to help get rid of her."

Crystal looked baffled. "There's a what-now?"

"You were crazy to start with," Mrs Pettigrew said with a sniff.

CHAPTER NINE

"*I*'m sorry. There's no excuse for my shouting at you." Crystal handed across a cup of tea to Emily, then stared at her empty chair. "Your friend isn't sitting there, is she?"

"No. She's still standing."

"Of course, I'm standing. This place smells like it needs fumigation. I bet the windowsills in the bathroom are black with mould."

Emily smiled. "I believe she's insulting your housekeeping." When an expression of alarm crossed Crystal's features, she waved her hand. "Don't worry. She insults everything about me all the time. I think it's her way of making friends."

"I don't need friends, thank you very much. Unlike everyone else in the world, I believe in being completely self-sufficient."

"How long has she been with you?" Now that the shock of the original explanation was out of the way, Crystal appeared to be taking things in her stride.

"She turned up late on Monday. It gave me a nasty turn.

I woke up in the middle of the night and she was staring down at me like I'd done something wrong." Emily laughed but the memory of her surprise made her heart thump a few quick beats.

"And she thinks someone murdered her?"

Emily nodded. "It makes sense. I'd be tempted if someone hadn't already spared me the bother."

"Hey. I'm right here, you know."

"Like I am when you say all the horrible things you do about me." Emily glared at the ghost until she turned her face away.

"She sounds like a real hoot." Crystal took a sip of her tea, shot it a concerned glance, and replaced the cup in her saucer. "Why can't she lead you to the killer and give you some secret information to make them certain she's talking to you? I'm sure I've seen that somewhere."

"In the movies," Mrs Pettigrew growled. "I'm glad this woman gave you the money back. I think the IQ of this table plunged when she sat down."

"It appears Mrs Pettigrew can't remember very much about the day or the murder itself. She does remember her head being hit and her stepson sitting in front of her, with his hands coated in blood."

"Oh, that does sound nasty." Crystal's mouth twisted in a strange smile. "Does she make you call her Mrs Pettigrew?"

"It's a sign of respect," the ghost said while Emily shrugged.

"It's the only name I knew to call her for a while, so it stuck."

"And Cynthia isn't her actual name, I suppose," Crystal said, twisting a fingertip into the deep dimple on her right cheek, a gesture of pure mischief.

"It's my legal name. Considering the forms and application fees, I'd be wild if I found out it wasn't," the ghost said.

"I'm happy with the names I know her by," Emily stated, a sense of loyalty rising. "And I'd rather this was a discussion over what to do than a dissection of her flaws."

"Sure. Just curious, is all." Crystal sat back, taking another large sip of tea and screwing up her face. "Sorry, I think the milk has turned." She stood up and cleared away her cup, leaving Emily's sitting on the table.

Emily took a cautious sniff, her own face twisting in disgust. She followed behind the medium, holding the cup by its handle over the saucer in her other hand. She didn't want to risk any of the foul brew falling on the carpet.

"And you call *me* rude," the ghost sneered. "Where're your hostess's manners?"

As Emily pushed through into the kitchen, she felt sorry to have raised the subject. It appeared that highlighting a fault of Mrs Pettigrew was the perfect method to have her magnify it to ten times worse.

"I'm sorry I yelled at you," Crystal said, grabbing the cup from Emily's hand to pour the mess into the sink. "Things have been tense in my community lately. It all came bubbling out in quite the wrong way."

"You were talking about a society. Did you mean the sceptics?" Emily asked, trying to remember that far back in the conversation. "Don't they approve of your profession?"

"No. I get gut feelings and intuitions about people. Always have, since I was a young girl. It's not good enough for the naysayers, though. They want facts and figures and data and proof. In my line that's not so easy to come by."

"Because you're a fake," the ghost called out from the other room. "You deserve any bad publicity you get."

"Isn't there some standard for your profession?" Emily

hadn't felt an urge to consult a psychic before and didn't know anything about the industry. "If you self-regulate, then it often stops outside forces poking their nose into your business."

"It'd be like herding cats." Crystal shook herself and the earlier smile made a strong reappearance. "And that's not why you're here. We need to figure out a way to turn your ghost from a liability to an asset."

"That would be wonderful."

"Your first problem is that, without any new facts, you're basically challenging the accepted view of this woman's death without any additional details. It won't be an easy sell."

Emily heard the laughter of the policemen in her ears. "I think that sums it up pretty well."

"If you don't have a bunch of new facts to put before them, the next best thing is to prove you're talking to a ghost."

"Perhaps there're some facts only she knows," Emily suggested, looking behind her where Mrs Pettigrew remained in the lounge room. She raised her eyebrows at the ghost who just continued to stare lackadaisically back at her.

"Can't she interact with things? A poltergeist is much easier to track than a simple spirit."

Emily shook her head. "When she touches things, her hands or whatever just go straight through, like the world is made of jelly."

"Peanut."

For a second, Emily stared blankly at the ghost, then she clicked her fingers. "Of course. When we went to her house the other day, her old cat reacted to her petting. Would that be enough?"

"It's a start." Crystal walked to the front door and slid it open, then looked back at Emily. "Well? Aren't you going to show me?"

"I really don't want anyone to see me," Emily said with a frown of concern. "It's the third day in a row I've been here. They'll think I'm stalking them."

"The footpath is a public space." Crystal gave her a hip bump. "It's not like they can call the police for you trespassing."

"No. They can just tell someone who'll tell someone and pretty soon my name will be mud." Emily wrinkled her nose. "Nobody's going to want to bring their expensive items into a charity store if they know the town weirdo's going to paw through their stuff."

"Like Pete isn't the town weirdo?"

Emily glanced at her, surprised. "Really? He seems fine to me."

"That's because you've met him after he broke up with Mrs P."

For a second, Emily thought the medium must be referring to her ghostly companion, then realized it was a reference to the kiwi slang term for a drug sold by points of a gram. Methamphetamine—P.

"I don't see my kitty anywhere," Mrs Pettigrew complained. "How'm I meant to show my existence if the cat won't oblige?"

Emily shook her head. "Perhaps we should try it another time. Cats like to go out as twilight comes on, don't they?"

Crystal gave a soft laugh. "It's only six o'clock. There're another three full hours of sunlight left before then."

"In which case, Peanut is probably sleeping," the ghost said. "Which is even less helpful because he always likes to curl up inside."

It took Emily a moment to remember Crystal wouldn't have heard that information. She relayed it to her, making a mental note to do the same in the future, minus the spurts of pure invective.

"How about we wander along the street rather than just standing and staring at this one house?" Emily said.

"Good idea," Mrs Pettigrew said. "That way the entire street can mark you down as a snoop instead of just my family."

Ignoring the bite of sarcasm, the three of them made their way along the side of the road at an amble. Even at the slow speed, it didn't take long for Emily to feel the familiar bite of pain in her hip.

"We can't keep doing this forever," she announced as her watch crept over to seven o'clock. "How about we head back home and think of another way?" Her stomach gave a large groan, adding its support to the idea.

"I suppose that's probably best," Crystal agreed with a touch of reluctance in her voice. "Though I don't know what else we can try."

"Peanut!" Mrs Pettigrew exclaimed, pointing. "See him? In the neighbour's front garden." Her smile of delight grew ragged at the edges. "Be careful. She never got on well with me."

"Just like everybody else, then?" Emily muttered under her breath, tapping the medium on the shoulder to point out the feline.

When Mrs Pettigrew hesitated, she jerked her head

toward the animal. "Well, go on then. It's not as though the neighbour's going to see *you*."

The ghost crept toward the cat, bending down to click her fingers. "Come on, Peanut. Come to Mummy."

As Emily and Crystal watched, the animal's ears twisted toward the sound and his eyes flicked to her deceased owner, then back to the patch of gravel where a sparrow pecked at the ground, unaware it was being stalked.

"Here, Peanut. You've been fed today already, fatty. Leave the bird life alone." Mrs Pettigrew clicked her tongue and fingers again, cooing nonsense syllables.

"Has she started yet?" Crystal asked in a whisper. "Or is she waiting for something else?"

"The cat's just ignoring her," Emily whispered back. "It's a pity her beloved pet wasn't a dog."

Despite Peanut's glare of warning, the ghost crept closer. At least the sparrow was immune to her progress, still happily pecking away at the patch of stony ground.

"Come on, kitty. Don't make Mummy look like an idiot in front of these people. You're a good cat, aren't you Peanut? Come on over and get a pat."

Peanut's hind legs tensed, then wriggled back and forth, calibrating his body for the impending jump. The moment his front paws left the ground, the sparrow startled and took flight, landing on the spouting above, well out of harm's way.

The cat sniffed where the bird had been, then cast it a disgusted stare and trotted over to his mistress. He rubbed his neck against her ankles and soon his back followed the rhythm of her strokes, arching to meet her hand.

"Do you see?"

Crystal nodded, biting the corner of her lip. "It's not all that impressive, is it? I can't imagine a policeman would be willing to reopen a case of accidental death based on this display."

Although she'd worked the same conclusion out herself, Emily's spirits took a short nose-dive. With each step she took toward the problem, the solution galloped a few more away.

Footsteps sounded on the driveway, and they turned towards a woman, holding a gigantic pair of clippers in her hand. The blades were dark with the juice of tree branches but looked hungry for meatier fare.

"What are you people doing on my front lawn?" the shrill voice demanded. "Do you know what we do to trespassers around here?"

CHAPTER TEN

"So sorry to intrude," Crystal said, stepping forward with her hand held out to shake.

The woman stared at the limb as though its very existence caused offence. "Who are you? Why are you standing on my lawn?"

"We're looking for houses in the neighbourhood," Emily said, nudging Crystal aside. "The property next door is lovely and just what we're after." She glanced around her as if to check for eavesdroppers and lowered her voice to a conspiratorial whisper. "I heard the lady of the house died and the current owner might be interested in selling."

"Lady?" The woman snorted but closed the clippers. She wiped her right hand on her trouser leg before shaking Crystal's offered hand. "I can tell you for sure, that was no lady, but it would be great to have some new neighbours. These are a nightmare." She demonstrated how much with an extravagant roll of her eyes.

Peanut must have caught her attention because the woman scowled at the elderly cat. "And don't even think about using my garden as a toilet again, old man. Go home and use your litter box. I'm not cleaning up after you again."

She kicked out at the animal, almost purring herself as Peanut skittered away.

"Old witch," Mrs Pettigrew said, sticking out her tongue. "Cats bury their mess. Unlike some people."

Emily shifted her weight from one complaining side to the other. "Have you ever been close to them? I wondered if you had any secrets we could use to negotiate to our advantage."

The woman looked over the fence, meeting the blank stare of the shuttered windows. "Come on inside and I'll tell you anything you want." She shuddered, then wrinkled her nose. "I don't get much in the way of company, these days. It'd be nice to have a chat."

Crystal practically led the way inside, eagerly taking up the offer. Emily followed behind with a tad more reluctance —the battle between extraverts and introverts played out in their differing enthusiasms.

"Am I invited, or is this going to be a full out attack on my character?" Mrs Pettigrew asked.

Emily shrugged, unwilling to respond in front of a third party and wishing she wasn't invited inside either. The ghost edged ahead of her through the doorway, apparently more intrigued than her question indicated.

"I'm Mabel," the neighbour said as she pulled out chairs and fussed until they were both seated. "Mabel Thistledrop."

Emily and Crystal introduced themselves and if Mabel recognised their names, she gave no sign.

"I got into a bit of a feud with the woman next door, I'm ashamed to say," she said while filling up the kettle and popping it on to boil. "When Cynthia first turned up, she was like a breath of fresh air for me and my boy." She gave a long sigh. "It didn't stay that way though."

"Did she say something mean?" Emily asked, thinking she'd probably done that at least once a day. "I heard she could have quite a rough edge to her tongue."

"My son died." Mabel busied herself pouring the boiled water into a teapot and getting cups out of an overhead cupboard. "It was a dreadful time. One day, he was complaining about a big bruise on his leg and feeling tired, the next he was in a hospital bed with leukaemia. He never came back out."

"How dreadful," Emily said while Crystal offered up tearful condolences. "I'm so sorry for your loss."

"Thanks. You'd think after twelve years, I'd be over it, but it still hurts just the same."

Emily looked out through the dining-room window to where the Pettigrew's house was visible over a wooden fence. "Was your son about the same age as Gregory?"

"Yes. Those boys loved to play together."

Mabel poured the tea and sat with them. For a long while, nobody spoke. Emily didn't want to stick her foot in her mouth with a tactless query and Crystal stared dreamily into the middle distance, lost in her own thoughts.

Even the ghost sat silent and sullen on the edge of the sofa.

"My Tommy loved Magnolia trees," Mabel said suddenly, the words appearing out of nowhere.

Emily frowned, wondering where the woman was headed.

"When he died, I got a tree to plant in his memory. It sat up near the gate in the fence where the boys used to duck through to play with each other."

Crystal shook herself out of her reverie, glancing over to Mabel. "I didn't see a tree when we came past."

"It's gone now." The woman gave another long sigh and behind them, Mrs Pettigrew gave a strangled cry. "It grew big and strong. The flowers were glorious each year. I loved those huge petals. Some days, I'd sit out there in its shade and think of Tommy and how much he would've loved it, too."

"What happened?" Emily asked, unable to resist a quick look over her shoulder at Mrs Pettigrew. The ghost's expression was sullen, her shoulders curling in, so she appeared twenty years more than her age.

"She poisoned my tree." Mabel's voice caught, and Emily glanced away as the woman struggled to keep her poise. "The petals all fell, almost overnight, and the leaves turned yellow. When I got a professional gardener in to examine it, he said someone had poured petrol over the roots."

"It moulted over the fence for years," Mrs Pettigrew said in a much smaller voice than usual. "I must've asked her a hundred times to trim it back. Those petals smelled like rotten meat when they fell in our back yard."

"I'm not usually the sentimental sort," Mabel said, rubbing her eye with a knuckle. "But on that day, it felt like Tommy had been taken away from me all over again. I couldn't believe she'd done something so awful but when I confronted her gardener, Abraham, he told me the truth."

"He'd poisoned the tree on her behalf?" Emily asked, wanting to be sure of the facts before she judged Mrs Pettigrew. She needed to be certain because there was a lot of judgment heading her way.

Mabel nodded. "When I explained, he tried his hardest to help revive the tree." She shook her head sadly. "But there was nothing that could be done. The petrol had been absorbed up through its roots a few weeks before the petals began falling. By the time I noticed anything wrong, it was far too late."

"I didn't know," Mrs Pettigrew said, her voice full of misery. "Until Abraham stormed in to tell me off and threaten to quit, I just thought it was a stupid plant she couldn't be bothered to keep in check. She was the one who stopped talking to me, you know. Greg and I missed Tommy as well, but Mabel just acted like we didn't even exist."

"I think that's the worst thing I've heard about Cynthia, so far," Emily said, telling the full truth. "Even if she didn't know about the connection to Tommy, to be so petty shows her up as a shallow, unthoughtful woman."

"Her husband Nathaniel just encouraged her," Mabel said, apparently deciding to let loose of all the venom at once. "Every time she encountered an issue, he always leapt to her defence. When I complained to him about the tree, he told me it was a trivial squabble that didn't affect him."

"He struck me as a very hands-off husband and father," Emily agreed. "When I was collecting all the boxes of goods belonging to his dead wife, he didn't once bother to come down and see me."

"As if that's the standard for being a good husband," Mrs Pettigrew snarled. "Making small talk with some woman from the charity shop."

"I wasn't at all surprised to hear around town about his affair," Mabel said in a tone of agreement. "Though, since she was carrying on with Abraham behind his back, Cynthia could hardly complain."

"It's all lies and conjecture," Mrs Pettigrew exclaimed as they took leave of Mabel's company. "Just because I flirted with a handsome employee doesn't mean I did anything else. I'm sure Nathaniel was no more fooling around on me than I was on him."

Emily felt the first pang of sympathy for the ghost as she made the claim. She imagined the fact they were divorcing did little to soften the blow.

"Did your ghost friend tell you any of this?" Crystal asked as soon as they climbed back into the car. "It seems she had a penchant for making enemies."

"As if everyone else in this township is somehow beyond reproach," the ghost said in a heated tone. "If you only ever listen to one side, of course, it makes a person sound bad."

"I think she knows her part in the killing of the tree was unforgivable," Emily said, staring straight into the ghost's eyes until Mrs Pettigrew dropped her gaze. "But she denies any inappropriate involvement with the gardener or knowledge of her husband having an affair."

"Though, I suppose just because she didn't know about it, doesn't mean he wasn't," Crystal said cheerfully. "The point of clandestine affairs isn't to broadcast their existence to your wife."

"I suppose it doesn't matter now."

"Unless the girlfriend killed her to get her out of the way. Or he did, to achieve the same."

"Except, she'd already asked for a divorce and Nathaniel had agreed. It seems a dangerous course of action when you're already getting what you want."

"Hm. Fair enough."

"This is the most ridiculous conversation I've ever heard," Mrs Pettigrew said, arms folded in a protective lock across her midriff. "Although, Mabel's babbling reminded me about the gate between the properties. I've thought the killers were restricted to those people in the house, but she could easily have snuck across, done the deed, then slunk back to her home once I was dead."

Emily pursed her lips. "Where is the gate located? Wouldn't somebody sneaking through there run the risk of somebody spotting them from inside the house?"

Crystal raised her eyebrows and Emily jerked her head toward the back seat. "Just talking to the ghost."

"It's right by the back door," Mrs Pettigrew said in a more thoughtful tone. "That's why it was great when the boys were little because they could run around in Mabel's back garden, then wipe their feet in the back hall before they trod mud all over the house."

"Not that having a secret entrance does us any good if you still can't remember what happened."

Crystal interrupted. "How did the police miss a murder, anyway? Didn't they sign this one off as an accident?"

"They did, and I'm not sure," Emily said, turning the car into the medium's driveway. "We've put in a request for the full coroner's report, but the librarian warned it could take a long time. Unless you know the family well enough to request a copy."

"You know, Hilda—the housekeeper—is in my felting club." Crystal struggled out of the car, then stuck her head back through the open passenger side window. "She's not much inclined to do anybody a favour, but I can always ask and see."

"That sounds great. Even if she's read through the report and can tell you some details, it'll be a big help."

"Well, then. We meet tomorrow night. I'll give it a shot."

Emily waved goodbye as Crystal mounted the porch steps, setting the wind chimes ringing.

"What a waste of time," Mrs Pettigrew said. "Remind me never to place any faith in your ideas again."

"You didn't have any faith in this one."

Emily reversed back onto the road, heading for home, then heard a suspicious noise from the back seat. With a penchant for safety born from the car accident, she pulled over and stopped the car before turning around to investigate.

"What?" the ghost asked as Emily stared between the seats, searching for the suspiciously familiar noise. "Keep driving. I want to get home, it's getting late."

She flapped her hands in Emily's face but that didn't stop her spotting the culprit.

"Meow," the elderly bundle of grey fur said.

Emily stared at the ghost and spoke in a flat tone. "You stole Peanut."

"He's my cat," Mrs Pettigrew insisted, folding her arms. "I didn't steal a thing."

CHAPTER ELEVEN

*E*mily wrung her hands together and stood back, surveying the cat to see if the hastily arranged setup would be to his satisfaction.

"Stop worrying," the ghost said, running a finger along Peanut's back. "Cats are practically self-sufficient. Peanut's capable of sorting things out for himself if you ever forget to feed him."

"Does that mean you forgot often?"

"Once or twice." Mrs Pettigrew glanced over when Emily gave a disdainful sniff—a strange role reversal. "Oh, what? Like you never skipped a meal. If he got all that hungry, the world is full of birds and mice, just waiting to be eaten."

"Only if he knows how to catch them. I'm not sure it's something we should encourage."

"Peanut can hunt them," the ghost said, giving the cat another long stroke along his back. "He's got the instincts of a tiger."

"How old is he?" Emily tried but couldn't keep the concern out of her voice. She remembered the doctor warning her not to keep an animal. *Pets and head injuries don't mix. Wait a few years until everything settles, then we can have another talk.*

"He's quite the elderly gentleman, nowadays," Mrs Pettigrew said. "Nathaniel let me pick him out as a wedding present, so he's the grand old age of fifteen."

"Oh, goodness." Emily felt behind her for the chair and lowered herself into it before she could fall. "Isn't that about two hundred in people years?"

"Years don't matter when your will is strong, and Peanut is the strongest cat I know."

Emily was only slightly reassured when she woke the next morning and found the cat had survived the night. "What about leaving him alone during the day?" she asked Mrs Pettigrew. "Aren't they meant to have someone keep them company? The poor thing might pine away to nothing, shut in here alone."

"I'm here," the ghost replied, an annoyed expression on her face. "He won't be alone."

"You're not coming along with me to the auction house?"

"It's your job, not mine." Mrs Pettigrew bent and chucked the cat under his chin. "My only task now is to look after this little fellow."

"And to remember who killed you. It would be good if you spent some time on that."

As Emily stormed out the door, she caught herself and had to laugh. She found the ghost so annoying when she was there, yet here she was, throwing a mini tantrum because the woman was staying at home all day.

"That's the goal, remember," she muttered to herself as she got in the car. "To get rid of the ghost and go back to getting your normal life together."

In the excitement of the past few days, she'd completely forgotten her goal to put her life back on track.

Pete was sneaking a quick ciggie outside the shop when Emily pulled up near the door. She tossed him a wave, then headed straight upstairs. Today, she needed to take everything scavenged from the boxes of donated goods to the auction house. The actual sale wouldn't take place until tomorrow, Friday, but the auctioneer assistant needed to check and tag every item today, ready to be sold.

Although her mind had been occupied by ghosts and cats last night, this morning Emily felt the nervous twist of trying something new. When buying and selling antiques had been a hobby, she'd never been too worried about making mistakes. The worst she could do was overpay for something she still thought looked nice.

Here, today, she might prove herself useless at her new job. That left her facing life on her ACC compensation, until she qualified for government superannuation. Although every worker in the country paid into the Accident Compensation Corporation fund expressly to be covered in Emily's situation, it still felt like welfare rather than insurance.

Besides, she'd never managed to save when she received a huge profit-share at the end of each year. At eighty percent of her base salary, Emily would struggle to manage. Especially now she couldn't even calculate simple bills.

"All those people are there to help," her neurologist had told her when Emily tried to explain the crawling sensation she got every time she needed assistance. "If you can't work out your finances, someone will help you. It's what they're paid for. It's the whole point of all these schemes. Likewise, if you need someone to help you read."

A shudder ran through her body now, triggered by the

memory. No, thanks. If it came to that, she'd find another way. Better to be a ghost as annoying as Cynthia Pettigrew than to live with such turmoil every day.

The array of signs outside the auction house were probably meant to inform, but they made her stomach pull into an even tighter knot. Emily knew her phone had a magic translation app for signs, but nobody had ever set it up for her and it was just another item on the long list of tasks she could no longer do for herself.

By following a man carrying an apple box stacked high with goods, Emily found her way into the acceptance suite. A woman with thick, blonde hair directed operations. When Emily turned up in front of her, she barked out, "How many boxes?"

That was something she could answer. "Four."

The thick brows lifted as they considered the one box held in Emily's grasp.

"I've left the rest out in the car."

The lady nodded and handed across four tabs. "Put these on the side and go over to table sixteen. Either I or somebody else will be across shortly to make a tally of items and offer spot valuations for the expensive goods."

Although she couldn't read the sign, Emily followed the direction the woman had pointed and placed her box in the centre of a trestle table. She guessed at the end of the day, they'd be collapsed against the wall to open the space for the auctions.

When the rest of the boxes were inside, Emily unfolded a chair leaning near the wall. The cry of thanks from her legs when she sat reminded her of Joanne, her physio. If she didn't stop wearing herself out, a lecture would soon come down the pipes.

"Hello again," the blonde lady said a few minutes later.

"I'm Sariah Channing. Are you the new girl working with Pete?"

Judging the woman in front of her to be aged thirty-five tops, Emily smiled to herself at the choice of phrasing. "Yes, I've just started this week so be kind to me." She held up her hands in surrender and the blonde woman laughed.

"I used to lend a hand down there sometimes," she said. "Before the current glut of over-donations, it was quite an exciting task to sort through the goods on the hunt for a bargain."

"But you don't go now?"

"You can thank Netflix for that." She held her clipboard out in front of her. "If an item in an op-shop doesn't bring you joy, let it go."

Emily laughed politely, with no idea what the woman was talking about. "Well, I hope these items have more potential than most to bring somebody happiness."

"Let's have a look." The lady pulled the box toward her and started to rifle through the contents. After a few under-the-breath exclamations, Emily felt more hopeful about her judgment.

"These are a wonderful selection," Sariah said after ten minutes examination. "I'm impressed that anybody would donate such expensive pieces."

"I heard sometimes people like to use the donations as a tax write-off," Emily said, parroting the information the librarian had told her.

Perhaps it was the wrong thing to say because Sariah's open face turned to closed, and she turned away. "I'll fetch some labels," she said, all enthusiasm gone from her voice. "We can get these tagged and ready for tomorrow. I'll send you back with an estimate but be aware we don't guarantee any of the valuations given."

"Oh, I'm aware of that," Emily gushed, wanting to make up for whatever faux pas she'd just committed. "I've participated in auctions before and I know there's no such thing as a sure thing."

Sariah drifted off and wandered back a few minutes later, dropping the labels and a marker pen on the table. "If you mark these up with your auction reference, we'll take it from there."

Emily stared at the pen, her head hot and her chest hollow. She poked at the side of one marker with her fingertip.

"Is there something wrong?" Sariah's momentary pique had passed, and she leaned forward, frowning. "Are you okay?"

"I'll need help with the labels," Emily said in a low voice. She checked behind her but the man at the next table was busy dealing with his own business. He didn't look to have spare capacity to butt into hers.

She rubbed the scar on her face, drawing Sariah's attention towards it. "I was in an accident and I find it hard to write these days."

The woman blushed, a strident colour change on her pale skin. "Ah, sure. I can help with that." She wrote the labels out, noting them on her clipboard as she did so. "Silly," she said, finishing up the task. "It's actually quicker to do it this way. I don't know why we never thought of it before."

She helped Emily to affix the labels, then gave her a large smile before heading along the line to help the next seller. As an afterthought, Emily pulled her phone out to take photographs.

She'd spent a long time on each piece, checking the ceramics for hairline cracks and comparing the creator's marks and stamps against books for confirmation of authenticity. It tugged at her to let them go, even though she'd known from the beginning they weren't hers to keep.

"I almost forgot," Sariah said, coming back over to Emily's table. "Here's your inventory for the auction items." She tore a sheet off the clipboard. "I keep the copy, but this is for your records."

"What happens tomorrow?"

"We'll load up an individual list on the website, so bidders know exactly what items are available. They can submit a bid online, but the actual sale won't take place until the auctioneer runs it tomorrow. Once that's done, we collect the money, deduct our fee, and in a few weeks pay your total earnings into the bank account on record."

"So, it's a standard auction, with the paddles and the phone bidding and everything?"

Sariah nodded. Emily hadn't taken part in many—even before the accident her nerves weren't up to the challenge—but she'd seen them enough to know the protocol.

Online auctions were more her speed. Submit your top bid and check back later to see if you'd won. Or trawling through a garage sale on the weekend, sharp eyes probing for a bargain.

"Can anybody attend?"

Sariah tilted her head to one side, a crooked smile playing out across her mouth. "Sure. Are you planning on coming along?"

Emily thought of the crowds of people there'd be—jostling for attention as they made their bids. Awful. "No, I'm just curious."

"That's good. We don't generally recommend sellers stick around for the actual auction unless there's something else you wanted to bid on. It can be a bit of a daunting experience and we've encountered a few problems in the past."

"What sort of problems?"

"People bidding on their own goods because they changed their mind or didn't think the other bids were high enough." Sariah shook her head, wide blue eyes twinkling.

"Oh, I'd never do that!" Emily pulled a face as her hand reached out to stroke the edge of the nearest box. "These don't belong to me to start with."

"No, they're from the Pettigrew estate, aren't they?" When Emily nodded, Sariah continued, "It's such a tragedy —the wife dying so young. Poor Nathaniel has been beside himself for weeks, now."

The tinge of warmth in Sariah's voice caused the hairs at the back of Emily's neck to stick up on end. She kept her voice modulated as she enquired, "Do you know the husband well?"

"Just through work. He's involved with the same organisation that our business sponsors." She nodded as though answering an unspoken question. "I feel blessed I've been able to offer Nathaniel some comfort during this extremely trying time."

Emily tried very hard not to stare at the woman. In the back of her head, Mabel's voice piped up, *I wasn't at all surprised to hear around town about his affair.*

So much for the ghost's staunch denial.

CHAPTER TWELVE

"I'm not sure what you're so worried about," Mrs Pettigrew said when Emily returned home. "I told you he'd survive the day."

Peanut wound himself in a figure-eight around Emily's legs, raising the concern he might accidentally trip her. When she opened the can of premium cat food sourced from the supermarket on a special trip, the cat gave that practice up and stared in rapt attention instead.

As Emily placed the bowl on the floor, Peanut lost interest in her and his old owner. He attacked the food in his bowl as though he hadn't been fed in weeks.

She walked through into the small dining room without incident and flopped into a seat. Her thigh muscles were twitching from the long period of standing at the auction house and she massaged them until the discomfort faded.

"I can't take care of him forever," she told Mrs Pettigrew in her firmest voice. "I'm on a limited income at the moment and those cans are over five dollars each."

"As if he's not worth five dollars, twice a day."

"It's not a matter of whether he's worth it. It's if I can I afford to keep paying that out and the answer is unavoidably, no."

"Doesn't your head injury qualify you for compensation? Or weren't you working at the time?"

"It qualifies me but I'm not happy living off public funds when I'm quite capable of working and providing for myself."

"Just not providing for a cat as well."

The two women glared at each other, Emily dropping her gaze first as she recalled her conversation with Sariah. It was hard to argue with someone when you knew something terrible about their private life. Something they either didn't know or had wilfully ignored.

"I'm taking him back tomorrow. If he's been at the house for fifteen years, then Gregory must be missing him terribly."

"Not enough to go looking," Mrs Pettigrew said, slumping into a chair in the lounge and glaring at the blank TV. "Well? Aren't you going to turn this thing on? I've been stuck with my own company all day and I'm bored out of my brain."

Peanut wandered through to join them, leaping into Emily's lap as soon as she sat. After a few minutes of clicking fingers and cooing didn't win him to her side, Mrs Pettigrew sat back with a disgusted expression on her face.

"Aren't you going to eat something? Or did paying for the most extravagant can of pet food rob you of the money for your own groceries?"

"I'm not hungry." Emily turned the television volume up a few notches higher and sank back in her chair. The warm purring body next to hers was comforting. It would be a real loss to send him back home.

Her stomach growled, and Mrs Pettigrew arched an

eyebrow. Fine. Emily was hungry but the thought of standing on her feet for twenty minutes in the kitchen while she cooked something made her hip ache.

If she hadn't made such a song and dance about expenses, she could have ordered takeaways but showing such hypocrisy to the ghost put her off the idea.

"Is this going to be our evening, then? Just slobbing in front of the telly?"

Emily glanced over with a raised eyebrow. "You're the one who wanted me to turn it on."

"Didn't you find out any new clues today?"

Yes. That your husband is having a fling with an auctioneer. "Nope. I've been working all day." Emily rubbed a hand over her eyes. They felt gritty and swollen. "I could search for some information about your husband's company." That wouldn't take much energy.

"What sort of information? Why would Nathaniel's company have anything to do with my death?"

"The librarian said he'd been hit with a massive tax bill. Perhaps he killed you for the insurance."

Mrs Pettigrew snorted. "Look if you want, but I doubt it. My life insurance has been the same measly hundred grand since I took it out in my twenties. Hardly enough to kill someone over. It would barely cover the expenses for a lavish funeral."

Emily tried not to think how much security the money would mean to most people, herself included. Instead, she pulled her laptop out and listed the search terms. She was overly familiar with the company registrar site so only took a few minutes to find the information she needed. When the computer read out the figures, she gasped.

"Two million dollars in back taxes? That's got to hurt."

Mrs Pettigrew leaned over to read the screen. "Hm. I'm

sure Nathaniel will've sorted something out. He's nobody's fool."

"According to the Inland Revenue Department, he's not half as smart as he thought he was. If you're clever, you do everything inside the boundaries of the law."

"What?" Mrs Pettigrew frowned. "Are you saying his company is acting illegally?"

"No," Emily admitted. "This isn't a fraud conviction just an indication he was skirting over the line. As long as he pays the bill, he'll be fine."

"I don't know why he hasn't already," the ghost said, concern edging into her voice. "Unless he's leaving it to the last minute."

"If he doesn't get it sorted soon, I guess he can kiss his company goodbye."

"They won't take the house or anything though, will they?"

"No, that should be safe. It's a limited liability company so they can only go after the company assets, not the director's private ones."

"Good. So, Gregory will still have a home to run to."

"Yes." Emily cocked her head to one side. "You really care for that boy, don't you?"

The ghost shrugged. "Not really. It's just if he doesn't have a safety net, that boy will fall apart. He almost did even with all the backing of daddy's money."

Emily wasn't in the mood for a rundown of the poor young man's faults. She snapped the laptop closed, then petted Peanut who'd startled at the noise. "Don't you worry, fella. I don't bite and neither does my laptop."

When Emily woke the next morning, the lower half of her body felt as though it had been run over by a truck. Again. She rolled onto her side and had to rest, panting, for ten minutes before she could think about swinging her feet to the floor.

"What's up with you?" her friendly neighbourhood ghost enquired. "You're moving like you're a hundred-year-old woman."

"That feels about right." Emily wondered for a few minutes if she should call Pete and let him know she wouldn't be coming into the store. One plus to working on commission rather than a wage.

Then she thought of the mountain of goods he'd warned her to expect for the day. Friday's were a clearinghouse as people ticked items off their list to free up the schedule for the weekend. The only day busier was Mondays, for the same reason in reverse.

Instead, she called into the doctor's office on her way and spoke to the nurse. It made her feel rotten asking for a repeat prescription on her pain medication. She'd hoped to at least make it to her next appointment.

As she waited for the duty nurse to check her details in the computer system, Emily thought about asking her to take off the auto-notification message to her physio. After the lecture on Monday, Joanne wouldn't be happy to see her still overdoing things four days later.

But that was the point of setting up the notifications. If everyone dealing with her medical issues knew everything, it aided her recovery. To hide this now, just to avoid another lecture, would push her into harm's way. And for what? As Joanne would no doubt tell her on Monday, it wasn't as though Emily listened to her chastisements, anyway.

As she walked out the door, Emily checked her watch.

The Evensbreak pharmacy in the nearby shopping centre would be open, but she decided to drop into the charity shop to talk with Pete since it was on the way.

With a coffee in hand and no customers, the early morning greeting stretched out for twenty minutes. When Emily finally tore herself away, she found a queue of people waiting at the chemist.

"You should go to the one on the other side of town," Mrs Pettigrew said, making Emily jump with her sudden appearance. "One of these pharmacists was so rude to me, I vowed never to shop here again."

"Mm," Emily said under her breath, wishing the ghost would stop trying to tempt her into talking when there were other people nearby. The longer she hung around, the less strange it felt to converse with her. Sooner or later it would spell disaster.

Although there was a row of chairs for customers to wait while their prescriptions were being filled, three elderly clients had already availed themselves. Emily turned to stare out of the glass frontage at the shopping centre carpark, hoping to distract herself from the pain in her legs.

Gregory loitered outside the chemist. His casual lean against a nearby lamppost appeared so staged, she assumed he was up to no good.

"Next," the pharmacist called out, and Emily walked to the counter. "That'll be ten minutes," the white-coated woman said. "We've got a rush on at the moment."

Emily nodded and looked around at the chairs. No luck. Three elderly bottoms were still perched on their seats. She could go back to the charity shop and take a seat there while she waited, but by the time she got back there and walked upstairs, the medication would be ready.

"What's he doing out there?" the pharmacist said in a tight voice.

It didn't appear she was genuinely asking Emily, but she turned to look. Gregory still stood outside, one pole nearer the door this time, his head staring in the opposite direction even as he edged closer.

"Right." The pharmacist strode out from behind the counter and slalomed through the line of waiting customers to reach the front door. "You're not welcome here," she shouted from the entrance, so loud everyone in the store turned to stare. "Get out. We're not selling you any drugs, not now, not ever."

Gregory's face turned as red as beetroot and although he maintained his slouched posture, hands shoved deep in his pockets, he moved out of Emily's line of sight. When the pharmacist returned to the counter, she was shaking her head.

"Has Gregory done something wrong?" Emily asked, unable to resist in light of Mrs Pettigrew's earlier comments. "He seems harmless to me."

"He's a scourge on our society, is what he is," the pharmacist said with a sniff, adjusting her horn-rimmed glasses. "Did you know, he used to get prescriptions for pills from the doctor up at the mall by faking illness, then sell them on to the other kids at university?"

Emily shrugged. "Yeah. I might've heard something along those lines."

"Well, we're the ones who filled those prescriptions. We didn't know there was anything wrong in doing that. It's not our place to second guess a doctor's orders. When the whole thing blew up, and he got kicked out of university, guess who his mother chose to blame?"

The answer was obvious from the indignation on the

pharmacist's face, but Emily still obliged. "She blamed you?"

"She did. Stormed in here one day shouting that we'd been handing out pills to minors, but the police would soon shut us down and that would be the end of our 'drug-dealing' trade." The woman mimicked quote marks as she said the words, her lips contorted with fury. "The chemist was packed full of customers at the time. His mother deliberately waited until midday, our busiest time, to come in and scream out her baseless accusations."

"Oh, that's dreadful," Emily said, clasping a hand to her chest. She sneaked a peek at Mrs Pettigrew who'd grown a sudden fascination with the row of hair conditioners lined up on the shelves. "I'd heard his stepmother could be quite unreasonable at times."

"Yes. I mean, god rest her soul and all that, but I swore from that day forward I'd never let her or that young man into this shop again. You know, even when the police came in and we showed them the scripts—all filled out and above board—she never even bothered to return and apologise for what she'd said. We still have folks coming in here and asking about it. A full year later!"

"She sounds like an absolute nightmare." Emily suppressed a small grin at her naughtiness. "Definitely not the type of person you'd want hanging around."

"Exactly."

"I just hope that Gregory got the help he needs."

"Oh, he wasn't an addict or anything like that," the pharmacist said. "Oh, no. He was just pulling off an act to trick the doctor and earn some money. I don't think he ever took a single pill himself."

"Really?" Emily frowned. She'd assumed from hearing bits of the tale from the librarian and here, that he must have been taking them, either through addiction or recreationally. "Why would he need the money when the family's so well off?"

Behind her thick spectacles, the pharmacist's eyes twinkled with glee. "They're not. The last I heard, the husband's close to declaring bankruptcy. His business went bottoms up and he mortgaged the house to the hilt to try to stave off the inevitable."

She gave a giggle, hiding it behind one latex-gloved hand. "He's probably going to end up destitute. No wonder the wife threw herself down the stairs!"

CHAPTER THIRTEEN

*T*he pain pills worked a treat but brought along with them the usual consequences. While at work, Emily struggled valiantly against the drowsiness, but the minute she was through the door at home she gave in to the effects.

Alas, within an hour, the doorbell broke her out of her dreams. On the other side of the door stood Crystal who squinted over Emily's shoulder to get a gander inside the house.

"Just come in, if you're that interested," she said with a laugh, opening the door wider. "I promise you, nothing in here bites." As Mrs Pettigrew bared her teeth. "Nothing alive, anyway."

"Are you sure you don't mind?" the medium said, walking through the hallway and into the lounge before she even finished the question.

Emily smiled and followed along behind the woman. Even though her nap had been interrupted, Crystal's enthusiasm was contagious, and she felt more awake than she had all day.

"Hello, Peanut." The woman bent to give the cat's tail a pull. "I guess someone smuggled you here."

"Did you see her do that?" Emily narrowed her eyes at Crystal, then shrugged. It didn't matter. "I would've taken him back to the family by now, but I fell asleep."

"Yes, I daresay they're missing the wee one."

"And it doesn't matter to anyone that I might be missing my pet?"

"No," Emily said, then blushed as the medium glanced over at her. "Sorry. I need to catch myself better. I had the horrible thought today I might start participating in a conversation with the invisible woman while I was out in company."

"Take this." Crystal rummaged in her bag for a minute, then thrust over a device on an ear hook. "It's a Bluetooth thingy for my phone but I don't know where I've lost it. The phone, that is," she hastened to add as if Emily might be confused.

"I'd clean that before you stick it anywhere near your ear," Mrs Pettigrew warned as Emily thanked the woman and popped it on the side table.

"Would you like a cup of tea or something?" Although the offer was genuine, Emily was very glad when the woman said no.

"I just popped in to say I talked to Hilda at my felting club last night. She can be a bit brusque but was in a good mood yesterday. Anyway, she said she'd look for the report and must've found it because she rang a few hours ago and said we can look at it on Sunday."

"Why Sunday?" Mrs Pettigrew demanded, and Emily relayed the message.

"The family attend church then, so she can count on them being gone half the morning. It should be enough time to read the findings and make a copy if we need to. Then she can replace it in Mr Pettigrew's drawer and he'll be none the wiser."

"Thank you for doing that," Emily said while Mrs Pettigrew continued to scowl. There seemed to be no pleasing her. It was a pity such a beautiful face was always so twisted up in one ugly expression after another.

She recounted the information she'd gleaned about the company and also mentioned Gregory's expulsion for selling drugs. "I don't know if they have any bearing on the situation at all."

"Or even if they're genuine," Mrs Pettigrew added, and Emily had to agree.

"How did the auction go?"

Emily gave a start, then giggled. "I completely forgot all about it. I guess we'll find out when they deposit the money in a few weeks."

"It'll just have started a few minutes ago," Crystal said, checking her watch. "If you want to go down there, I'll give you a lift."

"I don't know." Emily frowned even as her heart beat faster with anticipation. "The auctioneer who valued and labelled the items said they encourage sellers to stay away."

"Only so they don't feel so bad about accepting lower offers," the medium said with a big belly laugh. "If they can get away with something, you bet they will."

When Emily still didn't look convinced, Crystal leaned over and patted her arm. "We can stand in the back and hide behind some tall people. The auction house won't even know we're there."

Emily screwed up her face as though she was still considering options, then gave in to her desire. She desperately wanted to know how much the items would fetch.

Even if the bid price was disappointing, at least she'd know.

Better to have a reality check now than next week.

"Let's go."

Her enthusiasm lasted until Crystal pulled her car into the parking lot. When she saw the crowd of people hanging around outside, some smoking, most chatting, Emily felt shyness closing her throat.

"Perhaps we should just leave it."

"Don't be a sook," the ghost said, jumping out and heading straight for the door. "I want to see what sad sacks pick up all my precious belongings even if you're going to sit in the car."

Being shown up by a ghost wasn't how Emily wanted to end her week. She clambered out of the car, glad the pain pills were keeping the worst of her aches at bay.

"I'm usually at the electronic goods auctions," Crystal said as they walked towards the building. "The antiques and collectibles will be new for me."

Emily was about to ask why the medium needed electronics, then bit her lip to stop the question. Because she couldn't talk to the dead was the most likely answer. She wondered if there'd been a recording device capturing her every word when she paid her visit the other night.

Inside the building, the crowds thinned out. A lucky break because, otherwise, the room would have been stifling. Even with only a third of the seats occupied, plus a few stragglers along the walls, the air was muggy.

"Do you want to sit or stand back?" Crystal asked, peering brightly around the room. She waved a few times, and a man passing by gave her a friendly slap on the back.

"Sit, I guess." Emily pointed to where a large man, over six feet tall and almost as broad-shouldered, lounged on a chair. He was so big, the chair looked like it had been stolen from a primary school.

"Good choice." Crystal made a beeline for the row behind him, squeezing his shoulder as she moved into place. "Hey, William. Are you picking up something for your girlfriend?"

"Eh?" The man's face turned into a question mark. "Why would I buy Ellen anything? She's got money to do that herself."

"It's her birthday next week," Crystal said. "And if I'm not mistaken, it ends with a zero. If you want brownie points until the next one, take my advice and pick up something nice."

Will dug a phone out of his pocket and scrolled along the screen. He stopped on something, his face screwing up as he concentrated. "You're right." He rolled his eyes. "That's a lucky save."

"It's what psychics are for," Crystal said with a wink. "A little bird told me she might like a set of three ducks for the wall."

The man went still and stared at her for a long moment. "You're kidding, right? Because if you're not, I might have to have a long conversation about taste when I get home."

Crystal wrinkled her nose. "I'm kidding. Go off. Scavenge. Jewellery never goes astray."

As Emily settled into her chair, slumping down now her cover had walked away, Crystal called out to another person, then another. The woman might not be psychic, but she certainly had the pulse of the community.

"Ooh. It looks like they're about to start." Crystal waved over to Will and gestured for him to come back. When another woman tried to take the seat in front of them, she earned a nasty glare. "That's taken."

"Sorted," Will said in a whisper. "Remind me to shout you a beer the next time you're down at the Brumsby."

"You're on."

"I notice you didn't save me a seat," Mrs Pettigrew said as a complete stranger sat on top of her. She drifted up towards the ceiling, arms folded, a glare on her face.

The auction started to an atmosphere of good cheer. Some early items earned a small bidding war, but wins were easily conceded. There were plenty more goodies in the sea.

When her boxes were next on the lot, Emily pulled her phone out of her pocket. She could hear the auctioneer okay but come tomorrow, she'd be lucky to remember even half the selling prices of the goods. If she recorded the whole session, she'd be able to load the record into her computer and let it tally the whole thing.

"Careful they don't see you," Crystal said in a low voice. She was good at camouflage, not turning or otherwise showing she was talking to Emily. "Unless you're one of the authorised phone contacts, they frown on people having phones on in here."

"It's just to record things, not to place false bids," Emily whispered back. "But I'll be careful."

The sale of goods started, and Emily gazed upwards to see Mrs Pettigrew had an anguished expression on her face. Feeling as embarrassed as if she'd been caught staring, she looked at the floor instead. With the ghost's hard exterior, she sometimes forgot she was a person with real emotions and real regret.

Although the boxes were stuffed full of antique treasures, the auctioneer made short work of them. For most items, there weren't many bidders, and someone on a phone scooped up a dining set at a good price.

"Stay or go?" Crystal asked, leaning across when Emily's items were finished.

The earlier tiredness was back, drawing Emily's eyelids closed for longer with each blink. "Go."

She invited Crystal back inside when they pulled up outside her house, but the medium shook her head. "No offence but you look exhausted, love. Get a good night's sleep and treat yourself to something nice tomorrow. I'll pick you up on Sunday morning."

She waved goodbye and Emily opened the door to find Peanut impatiently waiting for her. For the life of her, she couldn't remember if she'd fed him or not until she peeked in the bin and saw the empty can.

"You're just trying it on, I see," she said to him, picking him up as she walked through to the lounge. "Come Sunday, if you haven't found your way back home, we'll take you for a car ride back to Gregory."

Mrs Pettigrew was silent as Emily switched on the television. After checking the news, discovering the world hadn't yet managed to blow itself up, she looked over, eyebrows raised. "I'm going to bed. Do you want me to leave this on?"

The ghost was lost in her own thoughts and it took a second before the question registered. When she turned to Emily, her eyes were dark pools. "Leave it off. I need to think."

CHAPTER FOURTEEN

*H*eat from the sun caused a trickle of sweat to gather at Emily's side and trickle down her back. She should move. There was shade under the trees to her right, but she couldn't be bothered.

Crystal pulled a bottle of water out of her bag. Condensation beaded on the outside and left a damp patch when she pressed it against Emily's arm. "Here you go. You look like you're getting far too hot."

Emily sat up, spinning off the cap and closing her eyes to better appreciate the trickle of cold water. After swallowing a few mouthfuls, she put the cap back on and held the bottle against the back of her neck. Bliss.

Earlier that morning, Crystal had shown up out of the blue, claiming she had no work on that day so was taking Emily out to lunch. They'd eaten at the Honeysuckle Café, with Emily ordering a plate of penne carbonara just to fly in the face of Mrs Pettigrew's hatred of carbs.

Okay, so the real reason was the pasta looked delicious and was crammed full of bacon, chives, and mushrooms, but the expression on the ghost's face made it all the sweeter.

Afterwards, they'd come along to the park, situated halfway along Pinetar's main road. The sun was bright overhead, and the grass had already given up its allocation of morning dew.

In a few hours, as the late afternoon settled into night, the public space would fill with teenagers—not wanting to stay at home but unable to afford anywhere better. The only signs of them now were the odd cigarette butt, tobacco or otherwise, and a crumpled can of a ready-to-drink concoction, catching and refracting the sunlight.

"Can you see her now?" Crystal asked, hitching herself up onto her elbows and crossing her ankles. The voluminous skirt she wore had pulled up, exposing half a calf's worth of unshaven leg.

"If I open my eyes. Do I have to?" Emily squinted, focusing on Mrs Pettigrew just in time to see her stare at the medium and draw a finger over her throat. "Yep. She's there."

"And how did you channel her to start with? Was it a sensation you got or a feeling like someone was watching you?"

A laugh burst out of Emily and she covered her mouth with her hand to stop another. "I didn't have a feeling, she was right there. The first I knew of her was when she shoved herself right up into my face."

"I've never shoved myself anywhere," the ghost demurred. "I just leaned over to check if you were breathing. When you're asleep, you look half dead."

"It must be a real treat to have such easy access," Crystal said. Her voice sounded wistful. "Often, I have to concentrate and use every trick in the book just to get a few tiny sensations or catch a word."

"That's because you're a fraud, dear," Mrs Pettigrew

said before yawning and rolling onto her belly. "I've met people who've gone into the wrong occupations for their skill set before, but you take the cake."

"I wish you could see and hear her rather than me." Emily closed her eyes again and dug her fingers into the grass. It was overdue for a cut. "The woman is exhausting."

"Only because you're so old," the ghost snapped. "I need to find a younger contact. You can barely walk sometimes."

Emily glanced over at Crystal. "She calls me Scarface, you know. Are you envious of that, too?"

An expression of such horror crossed the medium's face that Emily felt a glow of warmth in her belly. It had been ages since she'd last spent time with friends, not doing much of anything. So long, her mind had downplayed how good it felt.

"You speak of her as though she's the only ghost you've ever seen?" Crystal was pulling the petals off a daisy, eyes fixed on the task at hand. "Is that true?"

"Yeah." Emily shifted her legs, rolling so she didn't rest directly on her left hip, which gently throbbed. "Until she appeared, the only thought I'd given to the afterlife was gratitude I wasn't in it."

Crystal laughed and flicked the remains of the daisy away before plucking another one from the long grass. "Why do you think you can see her now?"

"Because I'm the first ghost worth the attention," Mrs Pettigrew said with a sniff at the same moment Emily replied, "It's something to do with her painting."

"Her painting?"

The quick scan from head to toe felt intrusive but Emily refused to shy away. It had been too long since she'd enjoyed the company of a friend to let her shyness drive Crystal away.

"When I unpacked her painting in the charity shop, that's when I think I dislodged her spirit, or whatever. Even Pete preferred it when I turned the image to face the wall. Her eyes seemed to follow us everywhere."

"Like the Mona Lisa?"

"But at a fraction of the price!"

They giggled, and Mrs Pettigrew stared at Emily as though she were touched in the head. "You know it's because of the accident, don't you?"

The sheen of sweat coating Emily's midriff turned to ice.

"It happened when the truck driver died, and your brain was being squeezed to a pulp."

Emily tried to force the memory away, but it swamped her, pulling her down, pushing into every inch of her senses until she was back in the car, part of the tangled wreckage, certain she was about to die.

***

"I'M SORRY," Emily said for the umpteenth time. "I don't know what came over me."

"Stop apologising," Crystal said, her voice light but her face creased with worry. "I've seen this sort of thing before. It's a panic attack, probably triggered by some type of post-traumatic stress. I'm the one who's sorry, prying into your history like that."

"You two can make a mountain out of a molehill," Mrs Pettigrew said with disgust, walking indoors and waving hello to Peanut. "You screamed for about two seconds, that's all. Once I went on a retreat to a mountaintop and yelled over the side of the cliff for five minutes every day."

"Would you like to come in for a cuppa?"

Crystal shook her head and placed her hand on Emily's forearm. "Tomorrow, maybe. After we go and visit Hilda. You get inside and rest, now. We've had enough excitement for the day."

No matter her denials, Emily couldn't help but feel ashamed of her behaviour in front of Crystal. Well, not just her, the entire park. She'd sent a bolt of panic through a young couple, pushing their three-year-old daughter on the swings. The poor parents must have thought a mad woman was on the loose.

For a moment, she was.

"I don't know why you're so concerned with what the fake medium thinks," Mrs Pettigrew said as Crystal drove away. "Surely, you understand today was all about finding out your secrets, so she can use them for her own gain."

"No, I don't." Emily put a hand up to her forehead. She couldn't work out if it was her fingers or her entire head that was shaking. The scar throbbed, begging to be touched, but she refused the siren call and dropped the arm to her side again.

"It's obvious. People like her, they're always on the lookout for someone to take advantage of. Usually, it's the sad sacks who come weeping to her door, wanting to know their dead Mum still loves them." Mrs Pettigrew screwed up her nose, lips thrust out in a monstrous pout. "With you, though, she struck a goldmine. Finally, somebody who can actually do all the things she's pretending."

"If you don't have anything nice to say, please be quiet." The phrasing might have sounded like a plea but the solid bedrock in her tone belied it.

The ghost shook her head but kept her lip buttoned, apart from cooing to her cat.

"Make sure you make him feel special tonight," Emily reminded her as she laid in her bed, despite the time being just past four o'clock. "We're taking him back to his real home tomorrow."

And we'll find out if all this snooping and prying has been worthwhile, she didn't say.

It was her own fault, Emily decided as she peered underneath the sofa. Her knees protested loudly on the way down, then again on the journey back up to standing. If only she hadn't reminded the ghost about returning Peanut back home, the woman wouldn't have hidden him.

Each time she glanced at the smug face, Emily knew that was exactly what Mrs Pettigrew had done.

"You'll be late," the ghost said as the clock made a beeline for a quarter to eight, the time Crystal had agreed to pick them up for the journey. "I mean, you're not wearing that around to my house, are you? It'll bring the whole tone of the area down."

Emily wiped her dusty hands on the front of her house dress and conceded defeat. She'd been calling to the cat since she first awoke two hours ago. Even the can opener didn't draw him out from hiding, and usually, he bolted straight for his bowl when he heard that.

"I hope you're happy," she said in a cross voice, her good night's sleep not having improved her mood much from a day ago. "Poor Gregory's lost his step mum and his cat only a few weeks apart. The poor lad'll be devastated."

The gambit to play on Mrs Pettigrew's affections didn't

pay off, and Emily turned to the task of what to wear. She settled on a long, flowing sundress covered in enormous flowers of red and yellow—the pattern much cheerier than she felt.

"Hoo-roo," Crystal called out from the front door, followed by a round of knocking. "I've just left the car idling, so I'll get back to it."

Emily grabbed her purse and phone off the counter and walked outside, taking satisfaction in slamming the door in the ghost's face. Not that it mattered to Mrs Pettigrew, who just walked straight through the wood.

"Oh, this is an earlier start than I'm used to, for sure," Crystal said as they joined her in the car.

"Sorry. I never even thought to say that we'd be fine going along to the house on our own."

"Never you mind." The medium pulled to a stop at the intersection. "It'll be worth it to get a gander inside the place. I've often picked Hilda up from outside or dropped her off, but she's never once invited me inside."

"Because we told her she wasn't allowed riff-raff," Mrs Pettigrew snapped, back on form from her earlier smugness. "Honestly, with the kind of friend that woman has, we'd be at constant risk of theft."

Emily flapped a hand at her for silence. "What's Hilda like when she's not at work?"

"Grumpy, when she's not just ill-tempered." Crystal grinned. "Most of the felting club is like that. It's not so much a circle of friends as a group of people who gather together once a week to talk about how dreadful the rest of the town is."

Emily burst out laughing, feeling the first hint of a good mood catching up to her. "It actually sounds quite fun."

Crystal hitched an eyebrow in her direction. "You should come along some time."

"I don't know the first thing about felting."

"You don't need to. It's easy enough to pick up the basics and what we're really there for isn't dependent on needlework."

"Yes, you should go." Mrs Pettigrew's voice was so snide it slunk around the car for a few seconds before weaselling into Emily's ear. "How else will Crystal pump you for information?"

Emily flapped her hand at the ghost again, wishing the gesture held the power to flick her away.

"I'll just park here," Crystal said as she pulled the car up to the curb, around the corner from the Pettigrew's house. "I think it's probably best if we wait until we know the family's left before we barrel right up to the door."

"If they come this way," the ghost grumbled. "It'd be a pity if they took any other of the dozen streets leading off Barbell Road."

It felt like winning a scratch ticket when Nathaniel and Gregory passed them by a few minutes later. Emily couldn't resist turning a beaming smile towards the ghost, only to find her looking resolutely away.

"Clock's ticking," Crystal said, starting the car and driving them the short distance to the door. "Let's see what the official reports can tell us."

When they walked inside, Hilda presented the same gruff façade as she'd done the last time she and Emily met—almost a week ago now she realised with a start. She bustled them through into the kitchen, obviously the place she felt most comfortable, and offered them a hot drink.

"Get her to make you a hot chocolate," Mrs Pettigrew insisted, face alight with pleasure. "They're the best thing you've ever tasted, especially for a diet drink. I lived on those over winter when I was trying to shed a few pounds."

Although a diet hot chocolate sounded appalling, the genuine enthusiasm threw Emily, and she followed the ghost's advice. Crystal thought it sounded divine as well, so they soon sat, cupping their hands around the hot drinks as though it were the middle of winter, rather than a warm morning in early summer.

On her first sip, Emily was a convert. "This is delicious. How do you make it so thick and creamy?"

"By using cream." Hilda reached back into the fridge and held out the clotted cream container. "This stuff's the best, though if you're in a pinch, pouring cream works, too."

"What?" Mrs Pettigrew's fury could be read in one word. She smoothed down the sides of her dress, her hands hovering a moment on the curve of her lower belly. "That sneak. She told me it was diet. No wonder I gained weight at the drop of a hat!"

Emily hid her smile in another big gulp of the chocolate drink.

"I'll go and fetch the papers," Hilda said. "Mr Pettigrew's kept them on his desktop since he received them. No wonder his business is in a slump."

She strode off, not a movement wasted as she collected a folder of paper and spread it out in front of the group. "Here we go. The report starts off with the summary findings, in the public interest, then goes back through all the details."

"Did the coroner spend a long time investigating?" Crystal asked.

"Goodness, no. I think he had a good idea just from the pathologist's report submitted after her autopsy." She shrugged. "You can see the date of the final opinion."

Emily looked over to Crystal who nodded. "It's from a week later." She held Emily's gaze for a moment, then turned back to Hilda. "Would you mind leaving us alone with the report? Only, we'll need some time to digest the results and discuss them. I wouldn't want to keep you from your job just to watch us do that."

"It's my day off," Hilda said, as though this explained why she could hang out with them.

After another second's awkward pause, Crystal inclined her head. "Then you must have a ton of things you want to get on with. How are you going with that new method for felting Glynda showed us? I tried it using an old bamboo bathing mat."

"I don't have anything bamboo. Besides, I just like sewing the patches together to form patterns. The smell of lanolin makes me too sick to start the entire process from scratch."

As Emily took another sip of her hot chocolate, Hilda finally understood the sub-text. "I'll head upstairs to get some sewing done, then. Gregory needs a set of name tags sewn into his new jeans."

"Yeah," Mrs Pettigrew said, full snark-mode engaged. "It's what all the cool young men are sporting this year. Name tags in the hem of their jeans."

When the housekeeper had left, Emily pulled her phone out and took a picture of each piece of paper in the folder. "I'd hate to think we get interrupted in a few minutes and lose our chance to read it through when we're this close."

"I don't think it's going to matter," Crystal said.

The expression on her face gave Emily pause, and she tucked away her phone. It was the same look her doctor wore just before he told her a piece of bad news. She'd seen it a lot in the past year.

She didn't want to ask but summoned up her courage. "Why? What's wrong?"

"The findings say your ghost friend was taking medication with dizziness as its primary side effect. There was no sign of foul play on the scene. He concluded she fell down the stairs, hit her head, and died."

CHAPTER FIFTEEN

"What a load of rubbish," Mrs Pettigrew exclaimed. She reached out a hand to turn the pages of the report, then issued a foul invective under her breath.

Emily chewed on her thumbnail for a minute, frowning. "And he was sure?"

"I don't know about all the doctor jargon but that's his finding. As Hilda said, he reached the conclusion so fast, it doesn't appear he was in any doubt."

"I wasn't taking medication," the ghost said, holding her hands out to either side. "At least, not that was prescribed to me. Occasionally I indulged in a few odds and ends, just to get a better response to life than my factory settings."

"Is that how Gregory got into prescription drugs?" Emily asked. She pressed a hand against her lower belly. A strange sensation was building there. Cold and hard. Despite the heat of the day and the warm drink she'd just finished, a shiver ran the length of her spine.

Crystal raised an eyebrow but kept her mouth closed.

Mrs Pettigrew didn't deign to give a response beyond a snort. Emily supposed that was another denial.

"What medication was she taking to cause the dizziness?"

"It's called Losartan. Apparently, it's prescribed to reduce blood pressure."

Emily giggled. "I'd have thought the people around Mrs Pettigrew would've required that more than she did."

"I don't remember taking these drugs." The ghost tilted her chin up and folded her arms. "Those are pills for old people. Not someone as young and vibrant as me."

"You're not young and vibrant, you're dead."

Crystal gave her a sharp look, then shrugged. "If you've finished taking photos, we should probably give these to Hilda to put away before she gets in any trouble." She shuffled the pages back together and shut the folder, hopping down from the chair. "Don't get into too heated an argument while I'm gone. The walls have ears."

She pointed toward the window and Emily saw the flash of movement as Abraham walked out of view. A flush crept up her neck from her collarbone. If he decided to tackle them for answers, she had no good reason to be here. That Hilda invited them wouldn't hold up since this was her employer's residence, not hers.

"You don't believe that, do you?"

Emily turned, her mouth falling open. Mrs Pettigrew's voice sounded nervous, anxious even. "Don't believe what?"

"That I fell."

She shrugged, pulling her mouth down at the corners. "I don't see how a coroner could tell the difference between a person falling down the stairs or being pushed."

"And I'm serious that I don't remember taking any medication."

"I believe you." Emily stared at the downcast figure. "But you don't have a lot of memories from around that time, do you? It's possible you'd begun shortly before you died, and it's just forgotten."

"Is that what happened with your crash?"

Emily pulled back, her hands rising to clench on a level with her chest. "There's the accident itself." The jolting warmth of spilled petrol filled her nostrils. Rich. Sickening. Pain crashed in on her from every side. "But the stuff for a few weeks before and after is gone."

"I guess given how long ago it happened, those memories aren't coming back."

"Yeah. I think they're gone for good." Emily bit her thumbnail, then forced her hand down to her side. "There's also the chance you don't—"

"Come on, then," Crystal said, coming back inside the room in a cloud of good humour. "Let's get out of here while the going's good. I can hear the call of hash browns, leading me astray."

"Sounds good."

"Ugh. More carbs."

"For goodness' sake," Emily said, rolling her eyes but feeling a rush of good cheer. "It's not like you have to eat them."

"You know, I'm coming around to the opinion that talking to ghosts isn't as sweet a deal as I might once have believed," Crystal said, looping her arm through Emily's. "Every time I hear part of your conversation, it makes me glad I can't listen to the other person's point of view."

"Rude!" Mrs Pettigrew stated in hot defence.

"Yes, you are," Emily agreed. "I think that was rather her point."

WHATEVER MOMENTARY AFFLICTION Mrs Pettigrew had suffered upon seeing the report of her death had lifted by the next morning. As Emily shifted boxes and cleaned the contents in search of treasure, the ghost kept up a non-stop stream of insulting guesses as to what the original owners could have been thinking to buy such worthless rubbish.

"Is there a printer around?" Emily asked Pete when she walked downstairs, before heading out to lunch. "I took some photos, and I'd like to grab some copies."

"For reading in bed later," Mrs Pettigrew suggested. A comment that earned her an afternoon of being ignored.

"Try the library," he suggested, and Emily felt like smacking her head. Of course.

"You're not going to spread those things around town, are you?" the ghost asked. "Because that's my private business, you know."

The thought had never occurred to Emily, but she took her pleasure in not responding. While falling asleep the night before, it had occurred to her she should ask a doctor about the findings and how they could be challenged. Since she had an appointment with her neurologist just before her physio session with Joanne, she might be able to swing it.

"I don't know," Mr Robertson said, his head nodding before his mind seemed to catch up with the fact he'd agreed. "Unless it overlaps with my area of expertise, it'll be a pretty general overview. No better than what you'd get with your local GP but a lot more expensive."

"She died of a head injury," Emily said, handing across the folder of printed images. "It struck a chord with me because of the similarities."

The neurologist sighed and took out the first page.

When he frowned, Emily held her breath, awaiting bad news.

"These aren't a coroner's findings," he said, taking her by surprise. Once again, the full force of her disability struck her. No matter how many ways she found around it, the sneaky handicap was always there, waiting to expose her as a useless old woman again.

"What are they?"

"It appears to be a list of items. Napkins and holders, a painting, a set of Wedgewood china." He scanned the list while Emily stared in confusion. "It's an accounting of household goods of some kind, but I'm not sure for what."

Mrs Pettigrew waved a hand in front of Emily's face to gain her attention. "Perhaps suggest he look at more than the first page," she said with a roll of her eyes.

"Are they all an inventory?"

Emily didn't give the ghost the satisfaction of sharing a glance with her when the doctor turned the page and his eyes lit with recognition. "Okay, here we go."

The man gave the report all his attention. Emily stared at her hands as he checked through the pages, clicking her fingernails against each other. The findings might be a wild goose chase but if it took up the entire appointment, it would grant her a reprieve.

At her physio appointments, Joanne was a nag and a nuisance. She was also easy to talk with and could relate when Emily had genuine complaints. Mr Robertson didn't have the same easy-going nature. He didn't couch bad news in an easy smile and a hand on the arm. He just delivered it in the same deadpan voice as he greeted her or asked her how she'd been feeling.

"This seems pretty straight-forward," the doctor said, closing the folder and pushing it back across the table.

Only five minutes. Darn it. That still left plenty of time.

"Is there a way the information could be wrong?"

Mr Robertson shook his head. "No, I don't think so. When she fell, the pattern of the stair left an imprint on the back of her head." He didn't appear to notice Emily's wince, raising his hand to touch the area in question. "If the injuries had been sustained another way, the wound wouldn't have that distinct marking."

"But she could've been pushed, couldn't she?" Emily clutched her hands together tighter until the knuckles protested. "There's no way of knowing if she slipped or if the fall was..." She paused, searching for a more delicate way of phrasing what she wanted to say. "Deliberate."

"She was prescribed a medication where dizziness is a common side effect. Her son heard her fall and found her at the bottom of the stairs." He paused for a second, then jerked his hand for her to return the folder.

"The prescription for the drugs was made a fortnight before the accident. That's a prime period for patients to display side effects if they're going to have a reaction to their medication. It was filled the same day as the script was written. There was evidence in her blood test showing she'd consumed the drug." He closed the folder again and pushed it back toward Emily.

"It might not be as exciting as someone shoving her down the stairs, but the evidence is compelling. I've no difficulty seeing why the coroner returned the verdict he did."

Neither did Emily. She still couldn't look at the ghost standing beside her.

"Are you happy with my opinion or would you like to stall on your tests for a while longer?"

Caught out. Emily gave a small smile. Today was the closest to human the neurologist had ever been.

"Good." He ran through the routine tests, having her touch her nose or tug on her ear, with her eyes open, then again when closed. She drew hands on a clock, showing the time as ten minutes to eleven. He had her peer in different directions and push her hand against resistance, up and down, side to side.

"And what were the three words I gave you at the beginning of the appointment?"

Emily opened her mouth to answer, the words sitting right on the tip of her tongue, then... Nothing. They'd gone.

She leaned forward, brushing a piece of imaginary fluff off her trouser leg. "Just a second, I'm feeling a bit hot."

"Mm. At the end of the day, the air conditioning sometimes gets a bit lazy."

"Come on. Answer the man so we can get out of here." Mrs Pettigrew said, walking over and poking her head through the door to look outside the office. "I want to see if Peanut's turned up yet."

Emily bit her lip, chewing at it so hard a metallic tang filled her mouth. She released it, not wanting to bite it clean through. There'd been an animal. A cat? Or was that just because the ghost had mentioned Peanut? One of the words related to something in the room. Furniture? Carpet? The lamp?

"I'm not sure I heard them clearly."

"Okay. That happens. Don't worry about it."

"Are you crazy?" Mrs Pettigrew stared at her. "Just tell him."

"I might schedule an appointment for a scan," Mr Robertson said, drawing his keyboard towards him. "It's been six months, so it's time we took another look in there."

"To check the bone fragments?"

He glanced over, frowning. "Sure. To see if they're moved."

The scar down the side of her face throbbed. Emily put a finger up to touch it, letting herself be seduced into running along its entire, crooked length.

"How does four-thirty on Friday suit you?"

"Good. I can finish up at work early."

The doctor pressed a button and a printer beside him whirred into life. "Here you go. I'll meet you there beforehand, this time. If I sit in the room while they perform the MRI it gives me a better feel for what's going on."

"What is going on?" Mrs Pettigrew walked closer, reaching her hand out toward Emily who jerked away. "Tell him the three things. He thinks you've got brain damage. Apple. Coin. Table."

A buzz started in the back of Emily's head. The lie about feeling too hot had morphed into truth. Sweat popped out on her forehead.

"Stop ignoring me, Scarface. Repeat the words. I need you out and about, helping to catch my murderer. Not locked up in a padded cell or dribbling into a hospital bed."

"What?" Emily raised her eyes, staring in horror at the man seated across from her.

The smile on his face slipped. "I didn't say anything."

"Apple. Coin. Table. Apple. Coin. Table." The ghost snapped her fingers between each word. "Apple. Coin. Table."

"Leave me alone," Emily shouted, turning on Mrs Pettigrew with a sudden explosion of rage. Her head swelled, her brain crushing to mush against the inside of her skull. "I don't need you yelling at me. If I wanted to tell him the words, I would. I can't remember them. If I don't know them myself, it's cheating."

"Don't talk to me! The doctor's sitting right there. He'll think you're crazy."

"I am crazy," Emily yelled. In a blinding flash of consciousness, everything slipped into place. It all made sense.

The skull fragments had shifted, pressing into a different part of her brain. How many times had the doctors warned her this might happen?

There was no ghost. There was no murder.

There were just boxes of goods in an attic room over the charity shop and no one to greet her when she got home at the end of the day.

"You don't exist," she whispered, staring as Mrs Pettigrew dissolved in front of her eyes. "You never existed."

As the neurologist ran around the table, calling for a nurse, Emily slumped in the chair. The world around her shattered as though her tears were made of glass.

CHAPTER SIXTEEN

*E*mily grunted as she pulled her leg up to her chest. "Just get it over with and tell me."

"Tell you what?" Joanne asked—her face a mask of innocence.

"Tell me that it's my own fault for overdoing it and you warned me repeatedly this would happen."

Joanne wrinkled her nose as a strand of thick blonde hair escaped its ponytail to fall forward and frame her face. "What kind of support buddy would I be if I always said, I told you so?"

"The type who's in the right while I'm in the wrong." Emily collapsed back onto the floor, her body protesting with a shriek from every muscle. "And that's the sort I need."

"Well..."

Emily raised her eyebrows.

"I seem to remember, I might have warned you about some consequences to your actions." Joanne held up palms up. "But it was all so long ago."

"At least enjoy it." Emily sat up and reached for a

towel to wipe the sweat from her forehead. "One of us should get something out of my complete mental breakdown."

"Considering you'd recovered by the time the doctor checked you into the hospital for an emergency MRI, I don't think it really counts as a breakdown."

Joanne held out her hand and Emily grasped it with a grateful sigh to pull up to her feet.

"I certainly hope it's the closest I ever get, anyway."

A shadow moved in the corner of her eye and Emily jerked around, but it was just the shadow of a patient walking on the other side of the windowed door.

"You seem a bit jumpy."

"Yeah." Emily finished wiping herself down and threw the towel in the wicker basket. "I didn't tell you but while I was"—she crossed her eyes and spiralled her finger around her ear—"I managed to steal a cat."

Joanne's eyes opened wide and a short laugh wheezed out of her.

Emily held a finger to her lips. "But I've grown rather fond of Peanut, so keep it a secret, okay?"

"Okay. I doubt the police will worry too much." The woman hesitated. "You didn't take it from a family with little kids, did you?"

"No. It was from the house of the dead woman." Emily didn't need to say which one. A flush warmed up the skin of her chest, then its crimson fingers crept a stealthy path up her neck until it reached her cheeks. "And he's really old. Fifteen."

"Well, you probably shouldn't keep animals at your stage of recovery but promise me, you'll set up a system so you never leave the house without checking his food and water bowl are filled up."

"I've done that," Emily said, running a hand through her sweaty, grey curls. "Not to mention the kitty litter tray."

"Good." The physio clapped her on the back. "On top of that, you need to remember to do the stretching exercises I gave you. With the tension you're carrying in your hips, your muscles are prone to cramping."

"I've been doing them every day. The poster is covering the television, so I don't forget."

Joanne searched Emily's face for a second, then gave a nod. "Okay. Since your neurologist gave your head a workup, I might get you into the hospital to give your body the same. We've got your group meeting in a few days, so it'll be good to cover all bases."

The meeting wasn't something Emily looked forward to, although she supposed she should be grateful. Every six months, the team looking after her physical and mental health met with her and the case managers in charge of her accident compensation.

They were meant to do it to come up with a plan to get her back into the regular workforce, but each meeting pushed that dream farther away.

As Emily walked out to her car, her mind worried at the idea of more tests. The worst thing was when a doctor said they were just routine—a red flag to show they thought something was wrong but didn't want to concern her. As though being lied to was somehow better.

A week ago, the trip to the hospital had been filled with pain and confusion. Mr Robertson hadn't accompanied her, but the nurse from his practice had travelled in the ambulance, holding Emily's hand until the paramedic moved her out of the way.

The rush of terror, that she might lose her cognition just because a piece of bone fragment had decided to take a trip, was overwhelming. Even now, beads of sweat popped out on Emily's forehead as her emotions relived the journey.

Somewhere on the jolting trip between the ambulance and the MRI machine, stored in the hospital's lowest floor, the fragment had slid back into its previous position. Crisis averted. Until the next time.

Although she'd never admit it to her doctors, Emily had held out hope the fragments in her brain might move, but she'd expected it to reopen the world currently closed to her. Just a fraction of a millimetre might leave her able to once again process written language. Turning her literate in a snap.

The fear they'd move and wipe out even more of her life hadn't been part of her considerations. Now, it stood out in sharp focus. The terror was stronger than the threat of death, to lose more of her abilities while retaining her cognition.

But life could be lived with fear without it incapacitating her. Emily drove home, relaxing as she pulled up outside her door.

Peanut greeted her with the loving admiration of a hungry belly. Despite his advanced years, he hadn't lost the kittenish habit of chasing after her, making walking a game.

Of course, she only had her mucked-up brain to tell her the cat was old. The white hairs on his belly might just be his natural colouring. With a can opener in one hand and the pet food in the other, Emily stared at the animal with a frown.

She didn't have to take the ghost of Mrs Pettigrew at her word since the hallucination only existed within her damaged frontal cortex. Unless she'd overheard the information elsewhere, she might have invented it.

"Perhaps I should book you a check-up with the vet,"

she said, reaching down to stroke a finger along the cat's back. It gave an annoyed flick of its ears. Dinner was no time to start doling out affection, there was work to be done.

How many other ideas did she have knocking around in her head right now that were just the result of her extended hallucination? The information about seeking a divorce came straight from the ghost's mouth. The vision of Gregory standing over his mother, blood streaking his hands. That came courtesy of her rude apparition, too.

Did Peanut even belong to the household?

For a second, Emily greeted the thought with hopeful enthusiasm—perhaps keeping him wasn't a crime—then she remembered. Abraham had cradled the cat to him and escorted him indoors. Definitely the Pettigrew's cat.

He also saw the cat reacting to the ghost's touch.

Emily shook her head. A nonsense thought. She'd found those popping into her head for the past week, too. Like a desperate plea not to write off her experiences.

But just because a cat acted funny while outdoors, didn't mean it was because a ghost was stroking him. Her mind had taken that real vision and inserted the spirit as an overlay on the scene, fitting what was already there.

Her phone vibrated, and Emily pulled it out. The snapshot she'd taken of Crystal Dreaming flashed onto the screen as it buzzed again.

Emily's thumb hovered over the green phone icon, then she switched and clicked on red. The image disappeared, retreating behind the home screen of Emily's fiftieth birthday celebration. She popped the phone back into her pocket and opened the fridge.

Although the medium had seemed like a friend a week ago, now Emily saw the truth. The woman had been hanging around to take advantage of her. Thank goodness she hadn't handed over any money, or she'd feel like worse of a fool.

If you didn't give her any money, how was she—?

Emily cut that thought off before it could gain traction. She was home. Her only job now was to feed the cat—tick—and feed herself. Once done, she could perform her stretches in front of the television, then reward herself with an episode from her favourite Netflix show.

Routine meant harmony. It meant getting a little better every day. If Emily kept to the path she'd been following, she should end up in a good place. Not the world she'd once belonged to—that was gone forever—but a good approximation.

When her work life was settled, and her medical concerns had faded into the background, Emily could consider making friends.

You wanted to go along to the felting club, remember? You said it sounded fun and Crystal's face lit up at the thought of your company.

No. Until the rest of her life was in place, there was no room for crafts and hobbies. Emily held her hands out and watched them tremble. These weren't hands that could hold a delicate needle, anyhow.

She pulled cheese, milk, and spinach out of the fridge, and grabbed the eggs from the kitchen bench. An omelette sounded good for tea. Cutting back on carbs couldn't hurt, not at her age.

When the phone vibrated ten minutes later, Emily turned it onto mute and placed it in her handbag. She didn't need distractions when her focus was on getting well.

CHAPTER SEVENTEEN

*T*he next morning, a Tuesday, Emily walked into work to find Pete standing by the counter with a concerned look on his face and a newspaper in his hand. "Isn't this your friend?"

Emily took the folded paper and squinted at the grainy newsprint. "Yeah. Crystal. Though, she's not really a friend of mine. I just met her a few times." She handed back the pages. "What happened?"

"It seems she held a séance for the wrong people," Pete said. "Do you want me to read it for you?"

"Nah. I'll catch up with it on my laptop while I'm working. Did you see the stack we got in yesterday?"

He nodded, his grin opening up wide enough to reveal his gap-teeth. "I think we can all thank the ground Marie Kondo walks on for that."

"Well, it better not continue." Emily knocked her knuckles on the counter. "If everyone's involved in the business of giving their stuff away, nobody is going to want to buy."

"They'll buy." Pete walked behind the counter, pacing around his stool a few times before sitting on it as though he were in the world's loneliest game of musical chairs. "Giving stuff away because it doesn't bring you happiness is a rich person's game. They'll tire of it soon enough and the rest of the population aren't in a position to even start."

"Well, that's a cheerful thought for early in the week."

Pete laughed and leaned forward, his arms folded on the counter. "It's good if you're on this side of the equation. The people keep coming and we get to keep serving them. Community spirit at its finest."

"If it earns me a living, I'm all for it."

"Speaking of which..." Pete pulled the keyboard out and tapped away at the keys, then gave a sigh. "Not there yet. Hopefully, by this afternoon."

Emily laughed. "You said that yesterday. And on Friday." She moved away and crossed to the stairs. "How about you just tell me when the auction house deposit actually turns up?"

"But it's the suspense that makes it so much fun!"

She would have answered, but the stairs took up her breath. The muscles in the back of Emily's legs didn't want to move this morning. The hard work she'd done in physio over the past year seemed wasted.

With the crush of donations that had arrived the day before, Emily hadn't done much besides stack the incoming boxes against the wall. She grabbed a box cutter now and began to slice open each one. Cataloguing these would take twenty-four-hour days if she needed to sort through each one.

Luckily for her situation, and unluckily for their recipient charity, many of the items inside were junk. In one,

Emily couldn't spot a single saleable item and ended up just strapping the top closed again in despair.

Why anybody thought a charity shop would need torn clothing and an assortment of tea cozies, she couldn't guess. Just because someone once paid money for a piece of clothing didn't mean it was worth anything at the other end.

"Oh, my," Emily said as she spotted her first real find of the day. "Look at this!" She pulled out the Royal Dalton mug, without a crack or blemish on it. The sailor depicted leered at her—an amazing feat between the squint in his eye and the pipe.

Emily turned, ready to show Mrs Pettigrew, then remembered. She shook her head, feeling silly, then swallowed past a lump in her throat. Suddenly, she wanted to be downstairs, talking things over with Pete, not stuck up here by herself.

She dragged herself to her feet before thinking twice and pulling over the laptop instead. The music player had some of her old favourites on there and she could set it playing, knowing she wouldn't hear a repeat for the rest of the day.

The computer opened on a browser tab, left on the paper's home page. Emily recognised the photograph of Crystal Dreaming again, the same as Pete had shown her downstairs. Before she could change her mind, she clicked on the article to have it read aloud to her.

"Crystal Dreaming has been the sole proprietor of the Rainbow Psychic Company for the past seven years. It's not the first name of the company, which has gone through sixteen variations throughout the life of its business. A startling number of changes for a standard enterprise, but the psychic assistance profession is anything but standard.

"In the last year, Crystal Dreaming's company has declared over four hundred thousand dollars' worth of 'donations.' Unlike a normal transaction with a set price and delivery, the service depends on word of mouth and repeat customers pleased enough with the outcome to continue paying hundreds of dollars for just a few minutes of work.

"And what is the work involved? For the two reporters who have been tracking Ms Dreaming's business model for the past eighteen months, it appears that is... Nothing."

Emily winced. Well, on the bright side, Crystal had been right to be paranoid.

As the article continued to play, highlighting the range of deceptive practices and abuses they suggested were the medium's stock in trade, Emily's emotions went on a tilt-a-whirl. She liked Crystal and enjoyed her company but agreed with some of the journalist's accusations.

If their original meeting hadn't gone pear-shaped with accusations flying, Crystal would have a few hundred of Emily's dollars in return for nothing. Not even a drinkable cup of tea.

The woman's self-delusion that she had 'feelings' and 'intuitions' she ascribed to another plane of existence was one thing, to charge clients an exorbitant fee to join in with that delusion, another.

Of course, Emily wasn't her customer. If it hadn't been for the hallucination of Mrs Pettigrew, the medium would never have entered her circle of consciousness.

One part of her wanted to visit and check Crystal was doing okay while the other said to leave it alone.

By the end of the day, Emily decided paying a short visit couldn't do anybody harm. Now she didn't have an annoying delusion of her own to drag around, it left her free to assess the woman anew. Any funny business and she'd be out of there.

To try to shake the stiffness in Emily's legs, she decided to walk around to Crystal's house. If she rested while the tendons were this tight, by tomorrow she'd barely be able to stand.

It meant by the time she turned onto the medium's street, she was tired and needed to rest. The crush of reporters standing outside Crystal's house sent Emily's stomach on a roller-coaster ride, and not one it enjoyed.

She slowed to a snail's pace while surveying the residence. If she tried hard enough, the gathered crowd would probably step back to let her through to the house. They might hurl questions or even unwanted opinions at her, but nothing she couldn't handle.

Except...

Crystal wasn't a close friend. She was just a person Emily had met a few times and gelled with. Not a confidant or soul mate to defend, even against the indefensible. The choice to drop by had been a poor one, and she turned and walked back around the corner, leaving the crowd of journalists and gawkers behind.

No. It wasn't Emily's mess. She didn't need to fight to clear Crystal's name or spruce up her reputation.

Except for the trickery of a skull fragment, Emily wouldn't even know the woman's name. Best to pretend that had never happened.

The flush of shame Emily felt as she arrived back at work to collect her car was just a foolish automatic reaction. A good night's sleep and she'd feel better.

"About time," Pete said the next morning. "I've been waiting and waiting."

Emily backed up a step, pulling at the top button on her blouse. "I'm not late, am I?"

"No, you're not late." Pete pushed across the screen, then blinked hard and pulled it back towards himself. "Sorry, forgot. We've got the money through from the first auction."

A burst of relief went through Emily and she hurried forward. "Do tell. How much did everything come to, added up?"

"Five hundred and eighty-five dollars."

The number seemed light considering the auction bids Emily remembered from the night, but it was enough to keep her going. "Not too shabby," she said with a smile, hiding the quick stab of disappointment. "Is that already transferred through to my account?"

Pete squinted, and Emily took a step back, warning bells sounding in her head. "That's my cut, right? You're not suggesting that's the total."

He screwed up his face. "Sorry, I should have worked backwards, shouldn't I? Yeah, it's the total for all sales, which gives you fifty-eight dollars fifty. I've already transferred it across."

Fifty-eight dollars? Emily couldn't swallow past the enormous lump in her throat. She'd spent more on cat food in the past week. It didn't make any sense. She remembered...

Emily's hand crept up to her scar, picking at the top of the twisted skin. "I can make that work, too," she forced herself to say. It wasn't Pete's fault her brain had gone on sabbatical during her first week at work. As a volunteer, he didn't get paid at all for working here. To complain about her earnings was shallow and self-indulgent.

"I'd better get upstairs and sort out another lot, then." She turned away, just in time to stop him seeing the sheen of tears in her eyes.

"No rest for the wicked," Pete agreed.

"Not even the extremely wicked."

CHAPTER EIGHTEEN

*E*mily lifted Peanut up from the laptop keyboard and moved him to one side. "Good kitty, but I can't have you blocking up the screen. Your new mummy's got work to do."

Mummy also wished she had an old ghost companion back who could read over her shoulder and tell her what the symbols meant. She hadn't thought of it when in the hospital a week ago, but that part of her hallucination was weird.

If the delusions were hers, then being able to read was her, too. With a mind split into two, Emily had become more of a whole person than she'd been for a while.

"If the doctor could work out how to get one part of that back, minus the other, it'd be good, wouldn't it?"

Peanut ignored her, stalking off to another seat. With his tail pointing in the air, he gave Emily a great view of his puckered rectum. He curled himself into a semi-circle and yawned so wide his head looked like a flip-top lid.

"Thanks for keeping me company, buddy. Why don't I take it from here?"

She had an earpiece in one ear, connected to her phone, while the other listened to the computer reading back information. Even though the process to transfer the amounts from one system to the other was painstaking, and possibly riddled with errors, it was the best Emily could think to do on her own.

"Of course, I could pay the librarian a visit. Or maybe the police officers would be in the mood to lend me a hand."

If her suspicions proved correct, Emily might well have to pay the police station a visit. Another reason to hope she'd been mistaken on the night and would soon prove her doubts wrong.

"Item 889A/17," the auctioneer droned in her ear. "A three-piece Georg Jensen Sterling Silver 925 S Pyramid Child's Place Setting. Designed by Harald Nielsen."

This was the one Emily remembered. She held her breath, wondering if she was about to be proven right, or shown up as mad.

"I'm bid six hundred and fifty dollars via phone," the auctioneer recited in his strange, fast monotone, and Emily gave a single sob of relief. Not mad. "Final bid, sold."

The gavel thumped, and Emily scrolled back to the start of the section. This time, as she heard the voice in her ear, she recited the words aloud into the computer. Next, she paused the phone and switched the earpiece to the laptop instead. After positioning the cursor on the line, she confirmed the same number was read back to her.

Only then did she copy and paste the words into her main document. So far, there were fourteen lines in total. Until now, they hadn't offered proof one way or the other, but the last bid cinched it.

The deposit into the bank account, even accounting for the fifteen percent fee the auction house was entitled to retain, was short. By Emily's reckoning, the list she'd painstakingly compiled now totalled over one thousand dollars. That put the deposit at a minimum of eight hundred and fifty. Not five hundred and change.

There was still another forty-five minutes of recording to go.

"Turns out your new mummy's not such an idiot," Emily whispered to Peanut.

The cat didn't care. He'd fallen asleep.

EMILY PRESSED a hand to her stomach as she walked into the library the following day. Her heart beat a fast rhythm and her legs shook, despite only having travelled from the car.

The night before, having listed out the items and obtaining a figure above eight thousand, Emily felt confident she could stride into work the next day and tackle Pete about the discrepancy.

This morning, her self-assurance had dissipated. The struggle to get showered and dressed took all her energy and she couldn't imagine replenishing it any time soon. She'd decided then to go to the library and ask the nice woman there to add up the figures, independently.

If she got the same result, Emily hoped her indignation would be enough to fuel her through the difficult conversation.

"Did you get a response already?" the librarian asked coming up beside Emily. "That's quicker than I expected."

It took Emily a second to remember what she'd been up to on her last visit. She shook her head. "No, I've got another task I need help with if you have time."

"I certainly do. On the computer?"

"Not necessarily. I need somebody to add up a list of figures and tell me the total. I've done it in my head, but I'd feel better if I could double check."

"At the computer, then," the librarian said with a smile. "There's no chance I could add something this long in my head. Despite my maths teacher always telling me that I wouldn't always be able to lay my hands on a calculator when I needed to, I think I've a much better shot at that."

Emily laughed politely as she followed the woman back to the computer desk. Her insides were now so twisted with anxiety, she barely registered the joke. "I don't want to take you away from anyone else."

It was the librarian's turn to laugh. "Does it look like I've got people queueing up for my services?" She waved a hand around the library, where apart from a few students with their heads buried in textbooks, there was no one to be seen.

"They might be hiding farther back in the stacks."

"If they're out of sight, they don't want me poking my nose in their business. Quite the opposite." She wrinkled her nose. "And don't get me started. I could tell you stories would turn your hair white."

"It's got most of the way there on its own." Emily put a hand up to touch her curls while the librarian brought an online calculator up on the screen.

"Do you want to go and search for some books while you're waiting?" the librarian asked. "There're some lovely graphic novels on the shelves over there."

Emily looked where the woman nodded and was about to decline when she registered the hunched shoulders. "What a good idea." She walked away, letting the librarian settle into her chair without someone staring.

It was a long time since she'd looked through books.

Even before they became useless to her, Emily had preferred to store them on the Kindle in her purse rather than taking up space on the shelves.

The first few books she pulled out showed action scenes. Men fought each other with gigantic shocks of lightning and fire spilling out all around them. The fourth book she opened showed a small girl instead, and Emily carried it to the nearest table.

Taking the weight off her feet was so wonderful, she gave a small sigh of satisfaction. No matter that she'd done her stretches religiously every day, the tendons in her legs steadily tightened. If the tests Joanne had scheduled for her later today offered insight into how to reverse that, Emily would be grateful.

From the pictures in the graphic novel, she worked out the thread of the story without needing the text. A warrior, albeit a very young one, armed with a formidable weapon to topple the large monsters inhabiting her world. She became so immersed in the story that it wasn't until the librarian touched her on the shoulder that Emily remembered where she was.

"Here're the figures I got," the woman said, handing across a note. "The total came to eight thousand, six hundred and sixty-five dollars." She clutched her elbows and hunched in her shoulders. "I added it up three times and got the same."

"Thank you so much for doing that," Emily said, leaning most of her weight on the table as she lifted herself out of the seat. "It's the exact same amount I got."

The librarian breathed out a sigh and let her arms drop to her side. "At least if we're wrong, we're both wrong, then."

"I now feel very confident we're right." Emily hesitated. "Can I borrow this book?"

"Sure," the woman said, her voice stronger now they were on more familiar territory. "Do you have a library card?"

Emily didn't, but that was a circumstance soon sorted out. She left the library clutching a few hours of entertainment that she'd long considered lost to her, along with her newfound assurance her addition was right.

"It's not that I don't trust the auction house," Emily took pains to explain to Pete. His chin jutted out with her first sentence and the tight line of his lips hadn't relaxed. "But I'm now sure these are the correct figures, so something's gone wrong somewhere down the line."

He pulled the list of numbers towards him and scanned them quickly. Emily hid her envy that the task that had taken her most of an evening to perform could be done in a glance.

"I've had someone else check them too," she said, pulling out the paper on which the librarian had written her figures. "Here. She came to the same total I did."

"The problem isn't the addition, I'm sure it's right." Pete looked at the new piece of paper but didn't touch it. "But this isn't the same list of items you took along to be sold."

Emily leaned back on her heels and frowned. She hadn't expected that response and her mind moved sluggishly to work out how to combat the new challenge. "I remember these items being in the boxes I took down there," she said. "I'm not sure what list you're talking about."

"The checklist." Pete stared at her, his face creased with annoyance when she didn't follow. He gave a large sigh and ran a hand through his hair. "Look, when you went to the auction house, they would have made you tag every item. Do you remember that?"

"Sure," Emily nodded, feeling a rush of relief. "The lady at the auction rooms helped me with that part." She clicked her fingers, searching through her memory for the name. "Sariah."

"Yeah, she's a good chick." Pete stared at the list of numbers, then put it on the counter and pushed it back to Emily. He reached down and pulled out a binder, then flipped through the pages. "She'd have given you a copy of the list while you were at the house, but she also scans through one to our computer. I keep tabs on all of that for the tax man."

Even though the charity held a tax-exempt status, they still had to account for every penny they didn't have to pay.

"This is from the week before last, right?"

Emily nodded and waited while he flicked through the pages in the folder. She still had the checklist Sariah had given her tucked away for safety in her wallet, but she was now so suspicious, she thought they might be very different records.

"Here we go." Pete pulled back the list Emily had meticulously assembled and began to cross through the figures. "These are from our charity. I'm not sure where the rest of the goods came from, but they're not from us." When he got to the end, he pulled out a calculator and ran through the crossed-out lines. "It's exactly as they declared."

Expecting an entirely different scenario, Emily pressed a hand against her churning stomach. Her vocal cords felt as though they'd be tuned to a higher octave. "I have a copy of the list. The one she gave me on the night."

She pulled it out of her pocket and handed it across, half-closing her eyes. Emily didn't want to see the look of realisation cross Pete's face as he understood somebody he trusted had cheated them.

But he glanced at the list, then pulled the computer printout from the binder. "I know you can't read the information on here, but surely you can see they're exactly the same."

He pushed the two sheets towards her, and Emily forced herself to look even though her head now thumped with an ache so strong her vision swam before her eyes. Flicking from one page to the other, she had to admit they appeared identical.

"Sariah must have given me the wrong list—"

Pete thumped his hand down on the counter. "Don't! I don't want to hear this. I'm sorry if the money didn't meet your expectations but I'm not going to stand here and listen to you bad-mouth someone just because you're disappointed."

"It's not that. I remember—"

"This was during the time you were hallucinating, yes?" Pete stared at her with a mix of anger and pity. Twin circles of red highlighted his cheeks.

Emily wanted to refute the very suggestion. She remembered everything about the day. She had a recording to back up her theory. Except...

She'd also thought she was talking to a ghost. She'd hidden in the back of the auction house because she knew she shouldn't be there. The recording might include items from her box, but it could just as easily belong to someone else. The numbers meant nothing to her after all.

Emily stepped back from the counter, shame rising to choke her throat and tears swimming in her eyes. It didn't matter. Whether Sariah had cheated her or if she'd just made a mistake in the midst of a delirium.

Either way, it was her brain at fault.

Either way, she couldn't do her job.

If Emily wasn't capable of realising someone was cheating her right beneath her nose, she couldn't continue to drag items along for sale.

If her brain had confused the events so badly that she'd concocted a theft where there was none, Emily couldn't even trust herself.

Her leg twisted, buckling beneath her. Pete rushed around from behind the counter to catch her and Emily fought against him. She didn't want his help.

But she needed it. For a few weeks, Emily had forgotten that she was a useless sham of a human being. She'd lulled herself into thinking she could rebuild her life when in truth all she'd done was drag down the people around her.

"How about you take the rest of the day off, okay?"

Pete's voice was so kind, even after his recent anger, that Emily began to cry in earnest. She wanted to tell him it was okay, she'd leave. He'd never have to worry about her muddled brain making groundless accusations again.

But the words weren't there.

Emily nodded and let him lead her out to the car park.

"Are you sure you're okay to drive? I could call you an Uber on my phone."

As though Emily could afford that expense on her new budget of fewer than sixty dollars a week. "I'm fine," she managed to choke out. "I'll just sit here for a while, then I'll head on my way."

"You've got those tests scheduled today, yeah?"

She nodded again. "And my case manager meeting tomorrow."

"Don't feel you need to hurry back in, okay? It's okay to

take a few sick days if you need them. That's the beauty of working this kind of job."

Pete thumped the roof of her car twice, then headed back inside, casting a worried glance back just before he closed the charity shop door.

CHAPTER NINETEEN

*E*mily sat in the conference room, feeling the stares of everyone as a physical weight. When she glanced up, four pairs of eyes flicked to other locations in the room. As she shifted in the chair and let her gaze drift to the muted taupe carpet, the weight came back again.

The conference room was far too large for their small meeting. Emily had nicknamed her case managers Tweedledum and Tweedledee due to their matching rotundness when they were first assigned. It had been so long ago, she'd forgotten their real names.

They sat at the head of the table, requiring Emily to limp the entire length of the room to reach her chair. Thanks, guys. With Mr Robertson the neurologist choosing a seat beside the managers, it only left Joanne the physio on her side.

"I'll fetch us all a drink, if you like," Tweedledee said, half standing. He looked disappointed when the group fed orders for coffee to him rather than waving him back into his chair.

Although Emily presumed he didn't have spikes of pain

jabbing into his hips, the man's rolling gait was worse than hers. If he fell onto his side, he'd bounce like a beach ball.

Tweedledum cleared his throat and linked his fingers together on the plasticky white table top. "We'll begin once Desmond is back," he said. "Is everyone having a nice week?"

Emily stared at the blank wall rather than answering his bland question. He wouldn't want to hear a genuine response and she didn't possess enough energy to come up with even the simple lie of, "Fine."

Her stomach was still tight with discomfort after her confrontation with Pete yesterday. When she'd thought of ducking into work this morning, before this appointment, it had shrivelled into a tiny ball.

"Are you doing okay?" Joanne asked with a concerned smile. "Your limp is worse this morning."

Of course, it was worse. Her muscles had atrophied at the same rate as her self-esteem.

"You'd have a better idea of that than me," Emily said. "Didn't the test results tell you anything?"

Joanne leaned back. The hand that had been heading for Emily's shoulder jerked away.

Hm. Good news, then. That made up for the medic sticking a needle into her leg muscles yesterday and leaving it there for over an hour.

"Here we go," Tweedledee said as he walked into the room carrying a tray of hot drinks.

Emily closed her eyes, trying not to hope too hard the man tripped, and everything went flying. Slapstick comedy would brighten up her day, but her mind was already in a funk without adding mean thoughts to its burden.

"Are you sure you don't want anything?" he asked

Emily. "We might not have a barista on staff, but our coffee machine is really good."

The temptation of sending him back to fetch her a drink that she wouldn't touch played across Emily's mind, then she shook her head. "I'm good." *Or, at least, I'm trying to be.*

"Right," Tweedledum said, opening a sheaf of papers that he didn't even glance at. "We've reviewed the progress reports from your health service providers"—he nodded at Mr Robertson and Joanne as though they might be in doubt as to whom he was referring—"and also spoken to your current employer."

Emily gripped the armrest of her chair. She hadn't expected that. The last time one of these excruciating meetings had been held, she didn't have a boss. "Pete Galveston?" she asked, unsure if he meant her co-worker. The actual person who'd organised her employment worked in Auckland and they'd only ever met over Skype.

"Yes, that's right."

"He's not my employer."

Tweedledum finally turned his attention to the papers, shuffling through them in a show of hunting out the information.

"He's a co-worker in the shop. I don't remember giving you permission to—"

"Here we go." The man cut her off by waving a piece of paper in the air triumphantly. "Yes, you told us he was a better contact since he'd be working with you day to day. When we spoke on the phone, Mr Galveston didn't seem surprised to hear from us."

"It's been a while since all of that was organised, hasn't it?" Joanne asked. "When you first contacted me to arrange handover from your physio in Christchurch, you already had the job lined up."

Emily's lower lip wobbled. *You forgot*, was what she was saying. *Your brain can't store information correctly, any longer.*

"Anyway," Tweedledee said, sitting forward. "How about we set aside the discussion of who gave permission for the moment? I'll make a note and if it's a genuine concern about privacy, we can return to it later. We spoke to your co-worker..." he waved at his companion to continue.

"Mr Galveston is mostly pleased with your work. He noted your attendance record is good and you've been very thorough while performing duties at the pace expected in your position."

Pete would never have phrased anything in his life using those words. Emily sat back in her chair, using the thumbnail of her right hand to push back the cuticles on her left.

She wanted to chew on one, but that would be a dead giveaway of her nerves to the rest of the table. Emily wondered what her colleague had really told them. *She's doing okay and turns up on time? Probably not.*

"He did express concern about an incident involving a third-party contractor for your workplace."

"You mean a woman who stole from us?" Emily sat forward, ignoring the concerned expression Joanne tipped her way. "Did he tell you how the auction house reported back goods sold at a fraction of their actual price? Did he mention she used my disability to her advantage, cheating a charity out of the entitlements at the same time?"

"He mentioned a lot of accusations, yes." Tweedledum closed the folder and clasped his hands together on top of the papers. "Would you like to take us through that incident?"

"It wasn't an incident." Emily pushed at her cuticle

hard enough to slice into the flesh. She curled her hands into fists instead, only relaxing them when she noticed Tweedledee noticing. "I have a record of the items I submitted to auction, and it doesn't tally with the written list the woman gave in return."

"Where is your list?" Tweedledum asked. His sickeningly sweet expression of concern did nothing to hide the glint of amusement in his eyes.

Emily's stomach jumped, and she pressed a palm against it. *Stay still, little buddy, we'll get through this okay.*

"I kept a record in my head. It's where I store stuff now that I can't write it down." She frowned, thinking back to the day of the auction. She'd forgotten in the interim but felt sure now there was another piece of evidence to back up her assertion. "I think I also took some photos."

"Were those the list of items in the coroner's report you showed me?" Mr Robertson asked.

With a start of surprise—he'd never spoken before in these meetings—Emily turned to him, eyebrows raised.

"Before you had the turn in my office, you showed me a report. It had an inventory of goods at the start of it."

She nodded, remembering now. "Yes, they might also show something." The papers captured in those photos had been in the folder the housekeeper had taken from Mr Pettigrew's desk.

Her heart thumped faster as Emily realised it might note everything donated to their office. Hadn't the librarian mentioned he was probably using it as a tax write-off? Mr Pettigrew must have taken stock before packing up the boxes.

"I think we're getting off track, here," Tweedledum said. He tapped his finger on the folder. "We're here to discuss your progress, or lack of it, and how it relates to your employment. Whether the auction house did or didn't provide an accurate list isn't relevant. The problem here is how you upset your co-worker."

"I didn't upset him," Emily protested. "The accusations did. He doesn't want to think badly of someone he's worked well with in the past. Of course, that's distressing."

"Mr Galveston indicated your behaviour during this incident was rude and aggressive." Tweedledum inclined his head on the last word.

Aggressive.

Emily flushed and gripped the armrests of her chair again. A memory flooded up through her, physically igniting different parts of her body in a unified expression of shame. If the chair had allowed her to curl into a ball, she would have.

When she first woke in hospital following the accident, Emily's mind had been as splintered as her skull. Keeping track of the cavalcade of new faces surging in and out of her room all day long had been exhausting. Not just that— confusing, upsetting, displacing.

If the pain from her body hadn't kept her immobilised, Emily would have walked out and never come back.

The one constant had been her best friend, Susan Tompkins. During her visits, every day at first, then settling back into twice a week, Emily calmed down. She understood the world, framed through her friend's eyes.

But her injury wasn't a stable thing, done and healed from. Although the surgeons had tried their best, a few bone fragments couldn't be dislodged from her brain. They were too close to important parts. Better to leave them alone and give her a chance at living than pursue them and leave Emily a vegetable.

It would be fine, if her body wasn't a living, breathing,

moving container. The lesions formed as her brain healed shunted the tiny bone fragments around, occasionally bumping them into concerning areas.

Just like her hallucinations of a few weeks ago, during her stay at the hospital a small shift had caused a change with large effects. Her paranoia had ratcheted up the scales until Emily became a living, breathing ball of self-defence.

Enemies everywhere. Liars stepping into plain view. With every new or old arrival in her hospital room, Emily saw a killer. One day she struck out before an assassin could claim her as a victim.

She had Susan pinned up against the wall, choking her. Emily mashed her thumbs into the woman's windpipe as hard as she could, desperation making her strong.

It took an orderly and three nurses to pull Emily off her friend. She hadn't seen her again. The courage to reach out grew larger and less attainable with every passing day where she didn't. It was a peak, insurmountable, and Emily couldn't work out how to take the first step.

Aggressive, had been the word entered on her chart. For a week afterwards, no nurse attended her without security backing them.

Emily understood the toll of hospital visits with no new avenues of conversation. She'd let her friends slide away from the commitment without raising a protest. They had their own lives. She didn't.

Susan had been the last friend to stick by her.

"Emily, if you want to take a few moments, that's okay." Joanne said. The rest of the table just stared at her.

"I'm fine," she snapped, turning to face Tweedledum. "Do you have anything else to add or is this just going to be a summary of events I already know about?"

"As you know," Tweedledee broke in, "these meetings

are to try to find an avenue for you back into the workforce. A report like this is concerning, but Mr Galveston didn't say your job was on the line. There are other matters of more pressing concern."

Mr Robertson cleared his throat and Emily looked at him, surprised. Speaking again? The news must be bad.

"I've analysed the results of the recent MRI and there's an indication some of your injuries are flaring up. We can't provide a definitive diagnosis but there's been enough of a change in function that it seems the pattern is toward decline."

Ah. Amongst all those unnecessary words, Emily deduced a nugget of information. "My brain function is deteriorating?"

The neurologist put a finger between his collar and throat, pulling the fabric away. "Yes. If the pattern continues, you may well lose more executive functioning. Already, there appears to be a significant change in memory."

"That might explain the incident with the auction house, then," Tweedledum broke in to say. "If your memory is playing tricks on you."

Emily blinked hard in frustration. The man didn't want to let go of his bone.

Joanne put a hand over Emily's, which still held the chair arm in a death grip. "I also hurried up the report from the nerve testing I made you go through yesterday. I'm sure you've noticed this change well before I have. There's neuropathy affecting your muscles, especially those in your legs."

The kindness in the physio's voice hurt Emily more than the diagnosis. Yes, she'd noticed how her legs felt stiff, even though she was doing everything she'd been told. Yes, physical movement became harder to perform, every day.

The care with which Joanne spoke heralded something far worse.

"What does it mean? For the future?"

Tears threatened, and Emily stared upwards. The fluorescent lights on the ceiling were encased in thick, pebbled plastic. One of a set of three in the space above Tweedledum made a tinking sound, like the hood of her car when the engine cooled.

"Without the nerves sending the right messages to your muscles, it will become increasingly difficult to move. They'll atrophy."

"Which will make it hard to get up all those stairs at work," Tweedledum added, a coda of doom. "Added to the poor prognosis from the recent scan, I think it's time we ceased to search for opportune work placements and prepared a program of continuing support instead."

"If you want to continue work," Joanne said, frowning across the table at the case manager. "There's no reason to stop until it gets to the point where it becomes impossible."

Emily stared at her, mouth slackening. Did she really believe those words were any kinder than what Tweedledum had just said?

"You're saying that soon, I'll be unemployable."

"It's not just that." Mr Robertson joined the conversation again. "Fairly soon, I estimate you'll require home care if you're to stay out of a facility. We should probably discuss those options now, so you can prepare."

"It's not the end of the world," Joanne said, unaware of the mushroom clouds obscuring Emily's vision.

CHAPTER TWENTY

*W*hen Emily arrived home after the meeting, she dropped her keys into the bowl, her purse on the floor, and curled up into a ball on the couch. The exercise chart hung over the television, as always.

She wanted to rip it off and tear it into little pieces. The energy to do so eluded her, and she settled for glaring at it instead.

"Useless old woman," she whispered to herself. "Can't even keep a job in a charity shop."

The involved discussion that followed the revelations had been lost on Emily. She half suspected that was the point of Tweedledum's organisation of the meeting. Give her so much bad news she couldn't concentrate, then make a host of decisions she couldn't keep track of, let alone participate in making.

"Ugh," she groaned and uncurled enough to lay flat on her back. The tears of self-pity stirred up by the discussion were still there, waiting, but Emily blinked them back again.

The car accident had cost her so much already, she'd allowed herself to believe it wouldn't demand payment of more. A foolish notion. It appeared it was out to steal everything and wouldn't be satisfied until she broke into dust.

Her friends were the first to go. Next was her job. She'd lost her home when it turned out her partnership agreement with the firm meant her actual salary to base compensation upon was tiny.

It had never mattered that her take-home pay was scarcely more than a junior staff member. Emily had grown used to budgeting out payments for her lifestyle, dependent on the profit share to partners, divvied out each end-of-year.

The qualifications that entitled her to those payments had never concerned Emily. The setpoint for numbers of new clients brought onboard, and the number of billable hours, was something well within her means to attain.

One sideswipe with a truck put paid to that.

Her benefits now were based on eighty percent of her salary. With most of her earnings tied up in a profit-share she could no longer access, Emily lost the means to pay for her mortgage.

The move to Pinetar had been partly generated by a wish to return to her roots, but more by the knowledge she could afford a house here. Her job mattered, too. The job everyone now thought she'd soon be unable to perform.

With a pulse of angry energy, Emily sat upright. The charity shop gig might soon dissolve away, but in the meantime she could right one wrong. If Mr Robertson had been correct, and there was a list of items inventoried from the donation, then between that, her recording, and the photographs, she might have enough evidence to prove the case. To Pete, at least, if not the police.

A few hours of painstaking searching and listening to instruction videos, Emily managed to connect her devices and programs together, so they'd read out the text contained in the photographs.

She sat back while the robotic voice listed items the charity shop had never been paid for. Her joy was only confused with the fact some items also hadn't made it to the donation boxes, either.

The gold-plated frame Mrs Pettigrew had insisted her painting originally came with was listed, not the second-rate timber painted gold that Emily had seen. The napkins should have come inside holders, listed as sterling silver 925. A tidy sum even if the work wasn't from a recognisable design name.

During the weeks spent doing her new job, Emily had taken individual photos on occasion along with the bulk lot at the auction house. She pulled those images up on her phone now, looking through them and comparing them to the listed details. A few matched and a few more didn't. Whoever had pulled together the original inventory had accounted for a host of things easy to sell, now mysteriously missing.

Emily could determine the differences but knowing who along the chain had performed the deed was harder. If Mr Pettigrew's money troubles were real, it could be him getting his deceased wife's estate to do double duty. A tax write-off on one hand, while realising the value of a lot of those items on the other.

But it could equally be the stepson. If the information about his involvement in the drug scene was reliable, he might easily have taken items to fence. If he travelled in those circles, it could be easy money or even a straight swap for product.

Hilda and Abraham also had access. If their jobs were on the line due to Mr Pettigrew being unable to afford the residence, perhaps they'd opted for their own private redundancy payment.

After switching between the most likely culprits for a good half-hour, Emily realised she didn't know any of them well enough to decide.

The Mrs Pettigrew she knew might just be a hallucination born of brain damage, but the real woman earned Emily's empathy. How terrible to be reduced to a pile of items with a series of thieves eager to enrich themselves.

The murder was a game Emily's mind had played with itself but given the terrible circle of folk surrounding the real Cynthia Pettigrew, it was plausible. With her thoughts mired in troublesome relatives, she moved the cursor onto the coroner's report and pushed play.

One of the problems with listening to a robot was the even cadence of the words. It was soothing, even on the parts where Emily had to struggle to work out the meaning because the emphasis went on the wrong syllable, producing an entirely different-sounding word.

The hypnotic pull had Emily firmly in its grip when the report came to a section outlining Mrs Pettigrew's prescription pills. The local doctor had written out the script, and she'd filled them at the Evensbreak Pharmacy.

Emily frowned, the information taking a moment to filter through to her subconscious where it triggered a memory. When the connection came, she sat bolt upright.

Evensbreak Pharmacy was the place where Mrs Pettigrew had told her the pharmacist had been so rude, she'd stopped going.

For a second, Emily paused, wondering if she could place any weight on a hallucination's speech. Then she remembered the pharmacist herself had verified the situation. She'd explained the deceased woman had chastised her about filling prescriptions for her stepson and never apologised.

The pharmacist had said Mrs Pettigrew wasn't welcome in the chemist after that.

Emily leaned over and fiddled until she could play the section back. Her ears hadn't mistaken her. The report stated the pharmacy that filled the prescription was the only place in town that wouldn't do it.

Listening to it for the third time, Emily began to chew her lip. This time, the information she remembered had come directly from the hallucination's mouth and nowhere else.

What on earth are all these squiggles? Mrs Pettigrew had said on the first night of their acquaintance. *This handwriting is even worse than my GP and Dr Pearson has a famously terrible hand.*

Dr Pearson wasn't the local GP. That was Dr Attica. Emily told the computer to search the yellow pages. It informed her Dr Pearson was based in Christchurch.

She sat back, puzzling over the two facts like they were colourful squares on a Rubik's cube. How did they fit in with everything else she'd learned about the deceased Mrs Pettigrew? Were they indications of a crime or did they just point to a sloppy investigation?

Evidence. The sergeant had been very clear he wouldn't take another look at the case without physical evidence. Did the wrong doctor writing a prescription filled at the wrong pharmacy count?

You're just avoiding thinking about your own position, one part of Emily's mind insisted. *Stop procrastinating and start to think seriously about your future.*

Oh, no. Her future hurt far too much for Emily to spend time on right now. She had the computer read the time out to her. Even though a million significant events seemed to have occurred so far today, it assured her it was only three o'clock.

Plenty of time to make a phone call to a doctor, just to check if a certain patient was still registered to their practice.

Emily already knew the privacy act laws would forbid the release of patient information. It didn't stop her pretending to be someone she wasn't.

"This is Mrs Pettigrew speaking. I'd like to make an appointment to see Dr Pearson."

She held her breath, half expecting the receptionist to be suspicious at once. Worse, she might ask a barrage of questions to confirm Emily's false identity.

"Can you spell your last name?"

No. Emily swallowed hard and channelled the spirit of her days-long hallucination. "Of course, I can spell my last name, dear. Can *you* bring up my file? I'm on a tight schedule here."

"Certainly, Mrs Pettigrew." The receptionist sounded apologetic. "What date and time were you after? Our first free appointment is at ten o'clock tomorrow."

"Oh, not that early. It's nothing urgent. In fact, I'm sorry to do this but somebody's just rung on the door. Can I call you back?"

She clicked the phone off before the receptionist could answer. Her heart beat so hard it made her throat click. A current patient, then. Unless the woman on the phone had been too rushed to check, they hadn't even crossed Cynthia off their patient list as deceased.

Surely, it was standard for the coroner to inform the doctor of a patient's death when they were their primary medical caregiver? You could only enrol with one practice at a time. Emily had gone through the process of re-enrolment when she first moved to Pinetar so her medical records would all be accessible to the local doctor here.

A doctor Mrs Pettigrew didn't usually see had prescribed her a drug she'd never taken before, and she'd filled the script at a pharmacist who wouldn't serve her.

Suddenly, the suggestion of murder didn't seem as farfetched, after all.

As Emily laced her hands behind her head and stared at the ceiling, her mind made clicks and connections, trying to fit together all the pieces of the puzzle she'd learned. When her stomach growled the first time, she ignored it, too intent on immersing herself in the new game.

The second time, Peanut joined in with the noise from her stomach, mewling from the kitchen door.

"Okay, kitty. I'll take a break." Emily walked through to the kitchen. If she remembered correctly, there was stir fry left over from yesterday. The confrontation with Pete had emptied out her appetite last night but the grumbling signalled its welcome return.

With a start, Emily realised Peanut's food bowl was already full. She picked it up, along with his water bowl, and frowned, sniffing at the contents. The edge of the food had hardened into spiky shapes.

It was the same brand of cat food, the same flavour. Yesterday, Peanut had eaten half of it before she finished pouring out the can.

"Don't you like this anymore, Peanut?" She reached out a hand to stroke his back.

Her fingers went straight through his fur.

Emily's vision darkened as she examined the cat. He nudged up to the edge of the bowl and tried to eat but his head just disappeared into the mess of food.

A ghost. Peanut was a ghost.

"Oh, no." Emily clutched at the neck of her blouse and spun in a circle, hunting for the physical pet. Maybe this was a mistake. Was she hallucinating again? Had her mind taken the confrontation with the case managers and worked itself into a tizzy?

"Peanut?" she called out as she limped into the hallway.

She checked in the laundry room where his litter tray sat untouched. He wasn't in the bathroom where a few days before he'd shredded an entire roll of toilet paper for his own amusement.

She was scared to enter her bedroom. The icy tendrils of suspicion that crept down her neck and up over her scalp were bad enough. She didn't want to turn it into certainty.

But there were no other rooms in the house to check.

Emily stood frozen in the hallway for as long as she could stand. When her legs insisted she move or collapse, she stumbled forward, lurching through the doorway.

The grey cat lay curled up on the bedspread where the morning sun would have shone. Emily lay beside the animal, stroking his cooling fur, her heart breaking into a million pieces while Peanut's ghost tried to curl into her arms.

CHAPTER TWENTY-ONE

*E*mily was still lying on the bed when the doorbell rang. She ignored it.

During the hours that had passed since finding Peanut, she'd fetched a large shoebox and lined it with a quilt he'd spent hours picking stitches out of. His ghost mewled in disappointment as she shut the lid.

Maybe ghost cat had a point. If Peanut wasn't going to cross over the rainbow bridge, perhaps she should keep the quilt out for his spirit to play with here.

The doorbell sounded again. Emily cast a sour glance at the entrance but refused to answer it. The decision was as much in the guest's benefit as hers. With her current mood, she wouldn't be great company.

She knew Peanut should be buried soon. Emily was torn over whether to do that herself in her own small back-yard or take the cat's remains back to his owners. She'd feel guilty to keep the cat to herself in death the same way she'd taken him in life, but also couldn't imagine turning up on the Pettigrew's doorstep with a cardboard coffin.

To throw her out on her ear would be the kindest response she could imagine.

A knocking came, this time a knuckle on her kitchen window. Emily turned a guilty scowl toward the sound, hoping the net curtains would shield her from prying eyes.

Abraham stood outside the house. The handsome line of his jaw might be the same, but the man's hair stood on end and, even through the masking curtain, his eyes were clearly bloodshot.

A jolt ran through Emily's body. Did he know about the cat already? Had it caused him a sleepless night?

She shook her head, following his progress as the man left the kitchen and headed around the back. He wouldn't get very far—a gate walled off the rear garden. Peanut had been alive yesterday. She was being silly, her emotions over-wrought.

The clear sound of somebody vaulting her back gate came to her. Emily rushed to the laundry room, peering through the small window at the same time Abraham cupped his hands around the glass to look in from the other side.

She jumped back, but it was too late. With a groan, Emily unlocked the door and opened it to her unwanted guest.

"Hey there, Miss." Abraham tipped his hat, then took it off to work the brim between his hands. "I'm sorry to barge in like this, but you're wanted up at the Pettigrew's house."

"Do you know what time it is?" Emily didn't. She'd lost track completely but guessed it must be seven or later because of the heavy blush of pink tinting the clouds.

"I do," the man said, shaking his head, "but it doesn't change anything. Please come to the house." Perhaps reading the reluctance on Emily's expression he dropped his voice to a pleading whisper, "There's someone summoning you there. She won't leave the rest of us alone. I don't usually stand for no truck about the afterlife but..."

His voice fell away completely, and he rubbed his eyes. When Abraham took his hand away, they appeared even more bloodshot than before.

"Cynthia Pettigrew is demanding you come up there, at once. She burned it into the grass with bleach. The letters are four feet tall."

ABRAHAM's garbled account of what had been happening at the Pettigrew household in the last week didn't leave Emily very much the wiser. She kept shaking her head, tracking the length of her scar with her fingertips, very much scared this was a newer, stronger hallucination.

If so, somebody would be along soon to lock her up and throw away the key. Time spent in a funny farm might be a respite from the tumultuous events of the past month.

"She never did like it when she couldn't get her way," Abraham burst out with just before he pulled the car into the driveway and Emily gasped.

Every window in the house appeared broken. Glass spilled out onto the windowsills and the gravel in front of the brick structure twinkled with hidden dangers. On the upper floors, where the ivy grew thickest, the green ropy strands held dozens of shards prisoner.

"What happened here?" Emily asked as she got out of the car.

In response, Abraham burst into tears. To see a man of such solidity and strength break down sent a jolt of fear plunging straight into Emily's heart. She gulped and turned her eyes back to the residence.

Curtains were smeared and streaked with dirt and paint. As she rounded the side of the house, taking care with every step, a viscous substance dripped off the flapping kitchen drapes. Blood was her first thought, but closer to, the unmistakable scent of tomato sauce allowed Emily's heart to settle back into its steady rhythm.

Hilda stood in the middle of the room, wiping her hands on her apron. From where Emily stood her hands looked to be the cleanest things in the room, so assumed the gesture was a compulsion.

"Oh," the woman said, raising her hand up to her mouth, then dropping back to the apron. "You're here! I hope you can get her to stop doing this."

Emily was about to ask what 'this' was, then a plate flew out of the cabinet, missed Hilda's head by a centimetre, and smashed into the far wall.

She hurried around to the door, opening it while Abraham followed along behind her more slowly. "I told you to wait upstairs," he said to Hilda as he passed her by. "Remember your blood pressure."

Emily ignored the two of them, focused instead on Mrs Pettigrew who stood in the hallway, waiting, hands on her hips.

"About time, Scarface. I have a score to settle and I need your help to do it."

When Emily opened her mouth to protest, a vase floated up from the side table near the door and hung in mid-air. Forgetting what she'd meant to say, Emily shook her head instead. "I spent all day today being bullied. I'm not about to accept the same from you."

The vase floated menacingly for a moment longer, then settled back into place.

From behind Emily came a mewing sound, then Peanut hopped into view. Mrs Pettigrew bent down, gasping in surprised delight, and the cat came running to leap into her arms.

"Good kitty," she whispered, her throat choking with emotion, then turned her attention back to Emily. "I suppose I should be angry with you for not taking better care of him." Mrs Pettigrew raised one eyebrow, tilting her head to one side.

"I tried," Emily began to say, then the ghost wrinkled her nose and laughed.

"I know you loved him, too. He just got a bit old."

"Unlike you." Emily stared at Mrs Pettigrew's face, consumed with love for her pet this time, unlike the façade of indifference she often presented. "I thought you were make-believe."

"Well, perhaps I am. If so, I'd like to be ten years younger and ten pounds lighter." The ghost smoothed her hands over the lean lines of her body. "Can you get your hallucination to do that?"

"I don't think so." Emily smiled. "And there's no chance I could dream up a phantasm that throws so many plates."

Peanut mewled to be let down and Mrs Pettigrew released him, eyes tracking him as he scampered to the stairs and placed his paws on the first riser.

Emily watched the two of them together and emotion stirred within her. For so long, the shards in her skull had been nothing but a nuisance. Now, she felt the potential for a different outcome altogether.

What had Pete said to her at work that first day? *You do the best with what you have.*

Emily didn't have the ability to read and write, and soon she might not be able to move around under her own steam. But she did have a lesion in her brain that opened a window into an entirely different world. As much as she'd tried to shut it or hope it would go away, she now viewed it in a new light.

She spun on her heel, spreading her arms wide. "I'll need a few more people to gather here if I'm to rid this house of your terrible ghost." She winked at Mrs Pettigrew, who offered her a smile of pleasure back.

"First off, I require the services of this town's finest medium, Crystal Dreaming. She's the only one who can assist me with understanding the spirit's intention. Someone needs to take me to her at once."

CHAPTER TWENTY-TWO

a huddle of reporters continued to crush up against Crystal's front door, eager for a short phrase or a quick snap. Emily sat in the car, happy to let Abraham face their probing questions and intrusive cameras while she slumped in the back seat.

After a few minutes, Crystal walked out, shielding her face with a newspaper. Perhaps not the best choice of cover considering it held her picture with a headline above it condemning her as a fraud. Still, the contents of the article didn't keep her from reaching the car and fumbling with the door handle. Emily reached over to let her in, and the medium collapsed into the passenger seat, panting from the effort.

"What's going on?" The expression of concern on Crystal's face dragged Emily close to tears.

She'd written this woman off, yet, in the midst of personal and professional upheaval, Crystal was only worried for her.

"The ghost is back," Emily said as Abraham started the

car and reversed out of the crowd of reporters. "And this time she's throwing a lot of stuff about."

"A poltergeist?" Crystal's face lit up with enthusiasm. "I've seen one before but not very powerful. She's actually lifting physical objects up?"

"She's pelting them at our heads," Abraham said in a gravelly voice, betraying too little sleep. "We were just about at our wit's end, then she demanded to talk to Ms Curtis. Mr Pettigrew fled to his company office and Gregory's cowering in the back of his wardrobe, afraid to come out."

"Leaving you and Hilda to deal with her?" Crystal sat back with pursed lips destroying her usually cheerful countenance. "I hope that man has offered to give you both a raise."

Abraham snorted with something near delight. "Good one. As soon as he's caught up with our back pay, I'm sure that'll be top of his mind."

"He's not paying you?"

"Mr Pettigrew's not paying anybody right now. He's scrambling just to keep the electricity turned on."

Abraham pulled the car over to the side of the road and turned back to Emily. "I won't lie. Part of the reason I contacted you when the writing on the lawn appeared was selfishness. If she destroys any more of that house, then he won't be able to sell. If he can't turn that property into cash, I'm going to be out of pocket. Two staff employed on a personal basis aren't going to have a look-in at money once the rest of his debtors make their claims."

"He's selling the property?" Emily shook her head, puzzled. She hadn't noticed any signs out in front.

"It's hush-hush. He's trying to liquidate the asset before the banks reclaim it as theirs. It's his last chance to get ahead of the mass of debt waiting for him." Abraham blushed as though suddenly realising he was telling tales out of school. "He's had it listed privately for months and that's the last I'll say on the matter."

He turned his attention back to driving and soon they were pulling into the Pettigrew's property.

"What do you want me to do?" Crystal asked, her voice clouded with worry as her eyes took in the scene. "I'm still unsure why you brought me here."

"Because you've got a group of people out to lynch you for communicating with those who have passed on," Emily said. "Something that I've decided to take personally. And you're my friend with a good head on her shoulders and enough experience of the world to be hard to shock."

"Really?" Crystal giggled. "You know, after meeting you I was tempted to throw myself in front of a car to see if I could get the same result as your accident." She paused and tilted her head to one side, giving a large sigh. "I decided, in the end, it was more likely I'd end up joining the lands of the no-longer-living rather than being able to communicate with them."

"I'm glad you didn't chuck yourself into traffic." Emily reached forward and squeezed her friend's arm. "The world would be a far duller place without you around. Now, do you want to meet a poltergeist with a chip on her shoulder?"

Crystal's face beamed as she met Emily's eyes in the rear-view mirror. "Yes, please."

AFTER TAKING her on a quick tour of the damage, Emily and Crystal walked back outside to talk to Abraham who refused to enter the house.

"If we're going to meet Mrs Pettigrew's demands and rid the place of her restless spirit, then I'll need you to fetch a few people here," Emily said.

"Mr Pettigrew, I presume." Abraham arched his left eyebrow in a wry gesture that set Emily's heart aflutter.

Her fifty-two-year-old heart, she reminded herself. The man couldn't be a shade over thirty-five.

"I'll also need Sariah from the auction house to attend, and Dr Attica. Mrs Pettigrew needs answers before she'll be able to move on, and they're the people keeping them secret."

Abraham nodded. "I can do that. It'll be a tussle to get the latter two to come along, though. You might need to give me an hour."

"That'll be fine," Emily assured him, looping her arm through Crystal's. "We've got plenty of groundwork to lay out before we can start."

When he'd gone, she turned to the medium. "I'm sorry I wasn't there for you when your story broke. It was selfish of me to stay away."

Crystal opened her mouth, poised to wave away the apology, but Emily shook her arm. "No, don't say it's okay. It wasn't. I'm only glad you were able to forgive me enough to come along today."

The medium inclined her head. "But what are we going to do?"

"We're going to stage an old-fashioned confrontation with all the suspects in order to unmask Mrs Pettigrew's killer."

The ghost appeared at Emily's side, making her jump. "Please, dear. If you're going to help find my murderer, the least you can do is call me Cynthia."

"Okay, deal." Another name flitted through Emily's

mind, the true name of the ghost standing before her. Mischief twinkled in her eyes for a second as she considered speaking the dreadful moniker aloud, then she bit down on her tongue to hold it still.

Perhaps earlier, it would have been okay. Now the ghost had become so strong, it could only end in disaster.

"Let's go and visit Gregory," Emily said, disengaging herself from Crystal to grab hold of the banister. "I can't believe his father left him alone with all this happening inside the house."

"Can't you?" Cynthia floated effortlessly up the stairs, an act that triggered Emily's jealousy. "Nathaniel's biggest skill in life is ignoring anything unpleasant."

"No wonder he let his company get into such a state."

Crystal tittered nervously. "It's so weird to hear you talk to somebody I can't see."

Cynthia grabbed hold of the vase sitting at the head of the staircase and waggled it from side to side. "What does she think of this, then?" she asked Emily. "Better?"

"Okay." Apparently intuiting the ghost's response from the movement of the object, Crystal hastened to add, "Since it looks like she means to do damage with that beautiful piece of china, I'll put up with not knowing where she is."

As Cynthia replaced the vase on the polished oak table, Emily frowned. She picked up the object and scrutinised its elegant curves. "This isn't beautiful china. At least, not original. It's a fake vase." She turned to the ghost. "Did you know that?"

"It was real enough when I brought it." Cynthia took it from her hands and turned it upside down, a grimace of distaste contorting her mouth. "You're right. This is some low-level knock-off. I wonder what else the household has been selling out beneath me?"

Peanut leapt up the stairs, jumping up to place his paws high on Emily's legs. "What's your problem, kitty? Do you know who sold the original vase?"

It appeared the ghost cat was far more interested in being petted than finding out the fate of a piece of pottery.

"I think he likes you now more than he does me," Cynthia complained with a pout. "It doesn't seem very fair considering how much time I spent with him."

"Short memory," Emily said, then at Crystal's raised eyebrows, explained, "We're talking about the ghost cat."

The medium burst out laughing. "That's one inexpensive pet, for you."

"Oh, yes," Emily said, returning her smile. "Peanut is the lowest maintenance cat you'll ever find."

Hearing his name, Peanut rubbed up against her ankles, staring into her face. If Emily wasn't mistaken, he now appeared younger than he had while staying with her. Death might have taken away his physical impact on the world, but it had restored his youth.

She glanced at Cynthia, wondering if her blemish-free complexion owed a debt of thanks to the grim reaper as well. Not that it mattered now, of course. There was a murderer to plan on catching and a young man's safety to check. Emily bent to stroke the ghost cat once more, then walked along the landing, searching for Gregory's room.

"It's the one at the end of the hall," Cynthia said with a note of remorse in her voice. "Please tell him I didn't mean to scare him. I just needed to get everyone's attention."

"You certainly did that," Emily said, unable to quell the note of respect.

She tapped on the door with one knuckle, not wanting to make too much noise if the poor boy was on edge. "Gregory? Are you in there? It's Ms Curtis from the charity shop and a friend."

For long minutes, there was no response. Emily was about to try again when she heard shuffling. Another minute passed, then the door swung a few centimetres inward. Gregory put an eye up to the slit.

Emily held her hands up, a gentle smile on her face. "We're unarmed, I promise. We just wanted to check that you're okay." After a second's though, she added, "Under the circumstances."

"Is she gone?" the young man whispered. His hair stuck up in an unruly tangle and his skin was ashen.

"No. I'm afraid your stepmother won't leave until she receives an answer to her questions."

The bloodshot eyes blinked slowly. "What questions?"

"About how she died."

Gregory stared at the carpet. After a moment's pause, he opened the door wider, stepping out onto the landing. "I don't understand. She fell down the stairs. Can't you just tell her that?"

"She thinks there's more to it." Emily hesitated for a second, then added, "And so do we."

His head was shaking even before she finished talking. "No. It's the truth. The absolute truth. I should know." He stopped, his mouth opening and closing as he gulped for air. "I'm the one who found her. There was a terrible racket, it sounded awful. By the time I reached Mummy, the stairs were covered in her blood."

Gregory's mouth twisted, and he tipped his head back, the twinkle of tears in his eyes. "I got it all over me as I tried to help her. When I pulled out my phone to call an ambulance, I couldn't type the numbers because I smeared blood all over the screen."

The tears flowed, gravity not enough of a force to stop them.

Cynthia snorted. "What an act. If I'd know he was this good at faking, I would've encouraged him into the theatre."

Emily turned a hard face toward her, then shrugged. If her suspicions were correct, they should be able to use the ghost's presence to prompt a confession from the gathered suspects. After laying her cards on the table, she hoped Crystal's heightened skills at empathy would help her to pinpoint the culprit.

But there were a few more factors to get into play if she wanted to cure all ills with one performance. She hooked her arm through Gregory's, leading him back downstairs, then turned to Crystal.

"Now, I just need to phone the press and let them know their favourite fake psychic is about to hold another séance. If we do manage to out a murderer today, it'd be good leverage to have the members of the press hanging onto every word!"

CHAPTER TWENTY-THREE

*B*y the time Abraham returned, ferrying the required attendees, Emily and Crystal had set up the house to their satisfaction. Although there'd been no knocks on the door in response to Emily's tip-off to the press, she had noticed a strange reflection from Mabel's next-door window, as well as a couple of bushes moving out the back.

"Come in," Crystal said in greeting to the new arrivals. She'd stripped off her jacket to show a long flowing dress, twinkling with sequins. Along with the large hoop-earrings that Cynthia had directed them to find in her old wardrobe, she looked even more like the charlatan psychic than she had when Emily first met her.

The guests and residents certainly looked askance at her outfit. Perfect. Set against the growing darkness, lit only by flickering candlelight, the effect of an old-fashioned séance was complete.

"Mrs Pettigrew has asked that you assemble in the main hall," Crystal said in a melodic voice. The initial effect might be jarring to the assembled family and friends, but Emily hoped it would soon become hypnotic.

"What does she mean?" Sariah asked in a pinched voice, glancing up at Nathaniel. "You don't have your wife's ashes in there, do you? 'Cause I can tell you right now, that stuff creeps me out."

"All will become clear, my dear," Crystal intoned. "Please just follow me through and take a seat. We hope to resolve this situation as soon as possible."

Dr Attica looked bemused. "I don't know what this is all about, but I've been at work since eight this morning. It'd be nice if I got a few hours rest and recuperation before I have to get up tomorrow to do it all again."

"Don't worry. We'll ensure you're well-rested."

Even Emily shivered at the strange menace hiding behind Crystal's tone.

When the new arrivals were seated, Crystal gestured for Abraham, Hilda, and Gregory to join them. Emily perched on the last chair in the row, clear enough for Crystal to see her but not drawing attention to herself.

"I've gathered you here tonight at Mrs Pettigrew's behest." Crystal raised a hand on each side, palms facing the ceiling. "The spirit has been restless since her untimely death and will become even more so with time."

"I don't like this, Nate."

"Silence!" Crystal shot a hand out toward Sariah and Cynthia followed her signal, sending a plate crashing against the wall above the auctioneer's head. "This is a matter of life and death. Each one of you played a part in Mrs Pettigrew's demise. Every person here has a case to answer."

Sariah began to sob gently, triggering a smile of satisfaction to cross Cynthia's face.

Nathaniel Pettigrew shifted on his seat, frowning at where Sariah's hand grasped his arm for support. "I don't know what you're talking about. My wife died in a tragic accident. Nobody is to blame except fate."

"Thank you for volunteering," Crystal said, walking close to the man until he jerked back in his seat. "We'll start with the role you played. Would you care to explain the financial state of this household?"

"No," Nathaniel said, standing and forcing Crystal back a step. "I would not. My financial situation is none of your business and I insist—"

Cynthia threw another plate. This time she didn't aim at the wall behind him. It hit her husband in the centre of his chest, driving him back into his chair.

The man's face flushed a dark crimson. "I don't know what game—"

"This isn't a game! This is a question of life and death. One person here knows the truth of what happened to Cynthia Pettigrew and it was no accident."

"I'm leaving." Nathaniel stood again, then hesitated as a plate floated in mid-air before him. "Whatever system you've got rigged up here won't impress me. I read about you in the papers. You're a fake and a fraud and I don't intend to listen to your rubbish for a minute longer."

"Was it the divorce?"

Mr Pettigrew stood very still, swallowing so hard it was clearly audible in the hushed room.

"I don't know—"

Crystal held a finger to her lips. "The prenup agreement must've seemed like such a good idea fifteen years ago. How were you to know that when it came time to pay it out, two million dollars would be enough to wipe out your entire fortune?"

He sat back down, legs shaking. "We weren't getting a divorce."

"Funny. That's not what she said." Crystal's sing-song voice delivered the classic punch line in reverse. "Cynthia assures me that when you denied her the funds for a private operation, she asked for a divorce and you agreed."

The medium tilted her head to one side, holding her forefinger up to her cheek this time, twirling it lightly in her dimple. "Did you think you'd be able to change her mind later? Were you so out of touch with your affairs you didn't realise the settlement would erase your entire net worth?"

"It wouldn't have made any difference except for the Inland Revenue and their joke of an assessment." Nathaniel's voice was low, but the fury was clear in his voice. "I had enough and spare to pay her to get out of my life. The idea of her leaving made me ecstatic. I would've asked her for a divorce years ago if it wasn't for Gregory."

The plate hit him in the crotch this time, avoiding damage by the reflective jerk of his hands.

"Yeah. That's a Cynthia move all right." Nathaniel's face screwed up, and he grabbed hold of Sariah's hand, holding it tight. "I didn't care if paying out the prenup wiped out my company and my assets. When I was twenty, I started off with nothing more than an idea and a hundred-dollar overdraught in my bank account. I built myself up out of nothing before. I'm not scared to do it again."

"You've been scared enough to sell off the treasures in this household, replacing them with fakes." Crystal raised her hands to each side again, opening her body up like a flower. "Is that how you got mixed up with this thief?"

Sariah flushed. "I'm not a thief."

"You've filed false reports for the auction house."

Emily stiffened as Crystal laid out the new accusation. Of all the information she'd stored up over the past few weeks, this was the stuff on the shakiest ground. To her credit, Cynthia appeared to realise this part of the trial was important to her. Crystal glasses smashed above the woman's head twice as she hesitated in giving an answer.

The second crash spurred Sariah. She covered her ears with her hands and screamed. "It was only a few thousand here and there. The rich fools who bring in their boxes out of their dead mother's attics don't miss anything. I only used it to help out Nathaniel. It wasn't for my personal gain."

"You cheated the charity shop out of thousands. Do you think you deserve a free pass, stealing from the most disadvantaged members of our community to keep a roof over your rich lover's head? He's not even paying his staff."

Emily shot a glance towards Hilda and Abraham, who both seemed happy with how the evening's entertainment was proceeding.

"I didn't know that! He told me the money was going towards his son's drug recovery."

Nathaniel flushed while Gregory appeared utterly nonplussed. "I don't have a drug problem."

Crystal swivelled on her heel, pointing her finger at his chest. "You certainly didn't have a problem selling them to young men and women. What habit were you feeding if it wasn't drugs?"

The young man sat back in his chair, crossing his arms over his chest. "It wasn't like it was meth or heroin. I just gave them a few pills to help them study if they needed it. No biggie."

"Big enough to get you kicked out of school."

Dr Attica was staring at Gregory so hard Emily

193

expected laser beams to shoot out of his eyes. She caught Cynthia's glance, and a cup went skidding along the floor to land at the doctor's foot. A signal they'd worked out earlier. Crystal turned to the man.

"You were the one pressuring the boy to keep selling more pills, weren't you? If it hadn't been for your bad influence, he wouldn't have lost his place at university."

The doctor snorted, looking unperturbed. "You're not blaming this on me. I prescribed the drugs to treat the boy's symptoms. I do my due diligence but it's not like I can run every young man or woman over the coals when they turn up with an obvious problem."

"An obvious problem that you're not qualified to diagnose. Or did you become a psychiatrist when the town wasn't looking?"

Dr Attica crossed his arms, nostrils flaring as he turned his glare onto Crystal. "The boy already had a diagnosis from a psychiatrist. It's on file at my office."

"Of course, it is. Nobody's accusing you of being unintelligent. I've no doubt at all you covered your tracks."

"I don't need to—"

Crash!

While they'd been talking, Cynthia had moved over to the line-up of chairs. With crockery running low on her side, she'd picked up a handful of broken pieces and dropped them, letting them shatter again on the floor.

"Stop it! Stop it! Stop it!" Sariah stood up, hands once again over her ears. Tears streaked her face and a bubble blew out of one nostril. "I'm sorry. I sold stuff and fiddled the reports. Please let me pay it all back. If it takes me another decade, I'll do it. I'll do anything. Just let me out of this place!"

Emily stood up, her guilt at the young woman's distress overcoming her need for revenge. "Come with me," she said in a soft voice, taking her by the elbow. While Cynthia rolled her eyes and poked a finger into her mouth, Emily walked the younger woman to the door.

"I hope you mean it about changing your behaviour," she said as Sariah staggered outside like a man freed after a thirty-year sentence. "You cost me a week's income and caused an enormous rift between me and my boss. If you're serious, I'd appreciate you coming to explain the situation to Pete Galveston tomorrow. Our charity runs three battered women's shelters from Pinetar to Christchurch. Your theft causes them actual harm."

Sariah nodded, backing up from the door while her eyes stayed fixed to Emily's face. Only when her heel caught in the gravel, twisting her ankle, did she turn away. "I promise," she said in a whisper. A second after she freed her foot, the woman ran, her heels striking sparks off the footpath as she ran up the road.

As Emily returned to the interrogation, Crystal was still haranguing Gregory. "Explain how you came to be at the base of the stairs, hands covered in her blood."

"Cynthia, don't!" Emily called out the warning as the ghost stood poised, a knife glinting in her hand. "Surely, you know this young man loved you. He didn't push you down the stairs. The blood got on his hands because he was the first one to reach you."

Mrs Pettigrew turned, frowning. The knife lowered, from above her shoulder, to chest height, to her waist, to her thigh.

"Except, he wasn't the first to reach you, was he?"

Crystal took a step back, ceding the stage to Emily.

With a nod to the medium, she ran a hand through her grey curls, inhaled a deep breath, and turned to the true suspect.

"Gregory's never been the first to anything in his life, has he, Hilda?"

CHAPTER TWENTY-FOUR

The housekeeper pulled back in her chair, her face a mass of confusion. "Pardon me?"

For a second, Emily felt the flutter of doubt in her chest. Before today, she'd never given the housekeeper a second thought. Like herself, Hilda had reached the age where nobody noticed her, even when she stood right in front of their nose.

Like herself, Hilda was more capable than society expected her to be.

"You take blood pressure medication, don't you?" A guess, but a reasonable one. Abraham had said as much when they arrived earlier to find Hilda cowering from the attacks in the kitchen.

"A lot of people my age take blood pressure medicine."

So true. Perhaps why Cynthia connected it so strongly with being old. The reason why she'd rejected the idea a doctor had ever prescribed the medication for her.

"When Crystal said she knew you from felting club and might be able to convince you to show us the coroner's report, I thought it was a long shot." Emily glanced back at the medium who had her hands laced over the expanse of her belly, a worried smile on her face. "But then, I didn't know at the time you'd engineered most of that report to match the facts of the case. You must've been so happy to present that to us. Anything to have us doubt the idea of murder."

"How was I to know you thought someone had murdered Mrs Pettigrew?" Hilda jerked her chin up higher. "Why would I ever think that? You were just some lady from the charity shop, poking her nose in."

"But I told you." Crystal frowned—the crease in her brow aging her ten years. "When we discussed it, I said my friend was convinced it was a murder rather than an accident."

"Did you?" Hilda shook her head. "If you did, I've forgotten. Are you sure that's what you said?"

"Dr Attica. Do you know the penalties of lying to the coroner?"

Emily turned her head around sharply, catching the man on the verge of drifting into a reverie.

"Eh? What's this?"

"Your name is all over the coroner's report. Prescribing medication to Mrs Pettigrew and signing her death certificate. A strange thing to do, considering she wasn't a patient of yours."

"Well, not now. She's dead." The doctor tilted his head back and looked down his nose at Emily. "I'm not sure you understand how these things work but Cynthia enrolled at my clinic the moment she came to Pinetar."

"Something both you and the ministry of health forgot to inform her actual doctor. I checked with his practice and she's still enrolled there. Nobody even bothered to tell them she'd died."

"It's a mistake." Dr Attica stood. "This evening has been a waste of my time."

"And yet you came." Emily planted her hands on her hips, mimicking the ghost standing beside him. "That's a bit odd, isn't it? A gardener turns up out of the blue asking you to come along to a house, with no real explanation of why. What did you tell him?" she asked, turning to Abraham.

"I said the family had questions about Cynthia's death. He turned pale, then bright red, then stammered an excuse why he couldn't, then followed me along to the car."

"Your behaviour's a bit odd, isn't it? For someone who was just the woman's secondary GP?"

"Primary. And no, I assumed the family needed help through their grieving process. It's a big part of a rural doctor's repertoire, helping the community come to terms with death."

"Nothing to do with Gregory's false prescriptions?"

Dr Attica scowled. "I've already said I know nothing about that. I've just been doing my job and if this family took advantage of my services, that's on them."

"Did you put the pills into her hot chocolate?" Emily said, switching her gaze back to Hilda. "Cynthia raved about the drink and insisted we try it. You must've laughed about that in the past, getting all that cream past her diet radar. How easy, to fill it up with pills to get your own back."

"You insisted she have a drink that morning," Gregory said, perking up at the words. "I remember Mummy said it was too hot, but you kept nagging."

"I did no such thing," Hilda said with a scowl. "You're misremembering things as usual. You're the one with the dodgy drug history. If anyone slipped medicine into Cynthia's drink, it was you."

"Except Gregory wasn't the one feeling ill from the side effects, was he?" Emily took a step toward the housekeeper, piercing her with a hard gaze. "You felt dizzy and she wouldn't even let you take the day off work, would she? Did you pop it into her mug to teach her a lesson? I'm sure it's no more than she deserved."

"Hey!" Cynthia's voice sounded wounded. "I am standing right here. You can choose your words a bit more carefully, thank you."

Hilda tilted her chin even farther up in the air. A few more centimetres and she'd be staring straight at the ceiling.

Emily held her hands out to each side. "I've only had to deal with her hanging around for a few weeks. I can't imagine putting up with her scorn and her harshness, day in, day out. Nobody will blame you if you just wanted to give her a taste of what it was like for you. It's still an accident, after all. Just a tumble down the stairs because the side effects made her dizzy."

"Is this true, Hilda?" Cynthia stepped closer to the housekeeper, poking a finger at the woman's chest.

"Ow." Hilda jerked away, her face turning frightened.

"Did you change the label on your own medication and pass it off as Mrs Pettigrew's?" Emily had already surmised that must be what happened but was glad when the woman gave the slightest tilt of her head. Hilda probably wasn't even aware of the gesture.

"What did you say to Dr Attica to make him help you cover up your tracks?" Emily stepped to the side as the ghost blocked her view of the housekeeper. "What did you have on him?"

"Yeah, what?" Cynthia poked Hilda in the arm.

"What's going on?" Hilda jerked to her feet with such violence, the chair overturned behind her. She turned in a complete circle. "What do you have rigged up in here? What tricks are you playing?"

"No tricks," Cynthia said giving a quick jab in Hilda's ribs. The woman bellowed in pain, doubling over though the blow didn't seem very hard. "That's just the feeling of Karma in action."

"This isn't a trick." Emily held out her hands and looked over to Crystal, who did the same. "We're not touching anything or controlling anything. Mrs Pettigrew is the only one acting out. We're just following her lead and asking the questions she can't give voice to."

"No." Hilda sobbed and ran over to the door leading to the kitchen. She pulled it open and Cynthia slammed it in her face.

"You're not getting away from me that easily!"

"Please, just admit to what you've done," Emily pleaded. "We can't control what the ghost will do to you. If you explain and beg her for mercy—"

"Beg her? Beg her!?" Hilda whirled back to face them. "I spent the last fifteen years begging that woman. For a decent wage, for time off, for her to raise her stepson so I didn't have to. I'm not begging anyone, anymore."

Hilda tipped her head back, scanning the ceiling, the walls, the floors, the staircase. "You hear that, you foolish, simpering woman! I'm done asking you for anything. I put the pills in your coffee. I thought you'd enjoy being the one too ill to do her work for a change."

Gregory and Nathaniel gasped, but Hilda didn't react. Her gaze continued to sweep the room, giving a cry of triumph as she spotted a levitating plate. She roared like a bull and charged toward the ghost.

Mrs Pettigrew didn't have to stand aside. The house-keeper sprinted straight through her. When she smacked into the far wall, Hilda turned and limped toward the apparition again.

"When you fell down the stairs, I thought, I can't believe I'm this lucky! The foolish woman who made my working life a misery has just killed herself. Serves her right!"

Cynthia howled and threw the crockery in her hand at the housekeeper as hard as she could. Hilda sidestepped neatly, the grace of a dancer contained in the move.

"Then I reached you and saw you hadn't hurt anything worse than your pride. A few bruises that would heal in a week. You cheated me."

Hilda raised her hand in a fist, shaking it at the empty air in front of her. "You should have had the decency to die in the fall. Instead, you opened your eyes and yelled at me to help you up."

The ghost took a step backward, her features turning into a caricature of distress. "I remember. You just stood over me gawping."

Emily opened her mouth to relay the message when Hilda gave a scream of frustration.

"Gawping, you said! I came over to help and you couldn't resist, could you? Any chance to toss me an insult, and you'd take it. You were a miserable, rotten cow and I couldn't live with you a minute longer. If I had the opportunity to do it all again, I wouldn't change a thing."

Hilda paused for a second, panting heavily. Then she grinned, exposing her sharp eye-teeth. "The sound your head made when I cracked it off the bottom stair is the most beautiful music I've ever heard."

CHAPTER TWENTY-FIVE

*D*r Attica tried to leave the house before the police got there, but to Gregory's credit, he stopped him at the door. "I don't think Hilda's the only one the cops will want to talk to." He dragged the man back into the room by his arm. "You have a lot of explaining to do."

As they waited, a flash from the stairs startled them. Footsteps ran back along the landing, and the sound of a man escaping from an upstairs window could clearly be heard.

"I guess that'll be the headline in the paper tomorrow," Emily said with a raised eyebrow at Crystal. "If they don't openly apologise, the press should at least move your expose to an inside column."

The medium grabbed hold of Emily's arm and gave a shriek of pleasure. Despite the torn emotions of everyone else in the house, Crystal appeared to be having the time of her life. "Wasn't that exciting?" she kept saying, whether anybody was listening or not.

Cynthia sat on the bottom step of the staircase, staring glumly at the point where her dead body had once lain.

Peanut wandered over, twirling in and out of her legs until he finally jumped into her lap. She stroked him, her face still as blank as it had been since Hilda's final revelation.

"We recorded the entire confession," Emily explained to the sergeant when he arrived to take Hilda into custody. "I don't know if it will stand up in court, but in addition to all these people's testimony, I hope it's evidence enough to reopen the case."

The sergeant lifted the digital recorder and peered at it as though it were a troubling foe. After a minute, he clicked his fingers and one of the attending PCs opened up an evidence bag. He tagged it and sealed it, looking disappointed all the while.

"What's the deal with the doctor, then?" the sergeant asked Emily after they moved Hilda out to the car.

"At the very least, he falsified evidence presented to the coroner. I think if somebody goes back through his clinical records, they might find a lot of incidences like that."

"We've got someone else down at the station, talking about you and your little soiree this evening." Sergeant Winchester said with a frown. "Sariah Channing. She's insisted on confessing to a long list of theft offences. Chief amongst them is swindling you and your charity out of about eight grand."

Emily felt a rush of concern. "I don't suppose you could let her work that off, could you? If you lock her up, we might lose the chance to recover that money, forever."

"No, you won't." Nathaniel Pettigrew stepped forward, looking a decade older than when he'd arrived at the house. "I'll pay any shortcomings out of my pocket. Since she handed the money straight to me, it's sitting in my bank account."

The sergeant raised his eyebrows but withheld any comment.

"Just a word of warning," Emily said, in the spirit of sharing. "We think a reporter was listening in to the whole confession, upstairs. There's a good chance it'll be in the paper tomorrow. If Crystal's house is anything to go by, that'll mean a clutch of reporters lying in wait at the station."

"We're used to that. I'm sure one of my PCs will be only too happy to keep moving them along." He sighed. "They'll keep coming back but it'll give one of those lads from the front desk something to do."

"Other than laugh at me." Emily still held a pocket of resentment for how they'd treated her when the ghost first appeared.

"Nobody will be laughing at you, tomorrow, I can guarantee that." He pushed a hand through his hair, deep creases radiating out from his eyes. "Besides, didn't I say, bring me evidence and I'll look at it?"

"Yes, you did." Emily wrinkled her nose. "It just wasn't in quite that tone."

"If anyone's interested in what I have to say, I can tell you to lock Hilda up and throw away the key." Cynthia stood up from her place on the stairs, clutching Peanut tightly to her. "What a nasty, vindictive woman. If only I'd known sooner, we could've been friends."

Emily stared at her for a second, then burst out laughing, much to the policeman's astonishment. Perhaps sensing volatility, Gregory pulled the sergeant away and led him over to where the doctor sat.

"Don't get me into trouble," Emily scolded. "Not when they've just started to show me some respect."

"That'll be fleeting enough."

Crystal skipped over to join them, her cheeks flushed and eyes twinkling. "Oh, my. I can't exactly say that was fun, but..."

Cynthia rolled her eyes. "Not so much fun from this side of the afterlife."

"I'm not sure what's meant to happen now," Emily said with a worried glance at the ghost. "Once Hilda confessed, I thought a door or a bright light might appear and guide Cynthia elsewhere."

"She's still here?" Crystal's eyes opened wide. "Now, that is very strange."

"Maybe I've just grown to love both of your company."

Emily hitched an eyebrow at her and was rewarded with a chuckle.

"Okay. I'll be good. If I'm still here when those officers leave, we can have a talk then." The ghost moved upstairs, Peanut hesitating for a moment, staring at Emily before following his mistress.

Gregory left the doctor in the care of the sergeant and wandered back to Emily's side. "We must all seem like horrible family members to you, I guess."

"Not really." Emily kept her eyes fixed on the scene in front of her rather than turning toward him. She was scared if she focused too much attention on Gregory, he'd lose the impetus to speak. "I haven't spoken to my brother since last year. How's that for terrible?"

"You don't get on?"

"We don't spend enough time together to know." She gave a shrug.

"Sometimes, I think I'd like to have a sibling."

Emily laughed. "I hope the rest of the time, you're grateful to be an only child. When I was growing up that was my one ambition."

"You were the older child?"

"No, the younger. I used to dream of Mum and Dad telling me that Harvey was adopted."

She heard a strange sound and turned to see Gregory with tears of laughter in his eyes. "Oh, boy. That does sound bad. And here I was thinking that being a lazy son with a troubled history was the worst possible outcome."

"You can't be all that bad." Emily's leg gave way, and she lurched to the side. Gregory's arm came out to support her and they moved to sit. "That's better."

"You were saying?"

"Your stepmother is one of the rudest and most heartless people I've ever had the displeasure of spending time with. But when she talks about you, it's with genuine affection."

"Really?"

Emily nodded. "Looks like the sergeant's about to head off."

Sergeant Winchester hadn't put handcuffs on Dr Attica but the grip he had on the man's arm didn't allow the doctor much leeway. He gave a nod to Emily before heading out the door and she supposed that was the best display of thanks she'd get.

"I don't know what to do now," Gregory said in a small voice. "If you get a chance, could you ask my mum if she has any ideas about what happens next?"

"What do you want to do?"

He shrugged. "I can't imagine getting a decent job without a university degree. I've left it too late to enrol for this year, even if another school will have me."

"Get a job." Emily smiled to take the sting out of her words. "There'll always be work available if you're really looking. If you can't get a paid job, try volunteering. Having experience along with whatever degree you're planning will put you a step ahead when you graduate."

Gregory nodded, his sad eyes travelling back and forward over the scene of devastation the poltergeist had wreaked. "I guess that makes sense."

Emily put a hand on his shoulder. "How about, for tonight, you don't worry about the future? Spend a bit of time with your dad and talk about what happened. It'll take a bit to process but it's best if you start in with that right away."

"You want me to talk to my dad?" A ghost of a smile played upon the young man's lips. "Somehow, I don't think that will be a success."

"Give it a try. He might surprise you." Emily grunted as she stood. Another indignity of growing old that nobody had bothered to inform her about when she was young. "And if he doesn't want to talk, know that Crystal and I will always be about if you need us."

"Yeah?"

Emily nodded. "Yes." She waved Crystal over to join them. "Now, I need to see what's happening with your step mum."

"Tell her I miss her."

"I will."

Together, Crystal and Emily mounted the stairs. Peanut trotted down the landing to greet them and Emily scooped him up into her arms. He stretched out a paw and caught a loop of beading on the side of Crystal's dress. She turned at the resistance, touching a finger to Peanut's paw.

"How strange. I can feel him." A beam of delight lit up the medium's face. "This is your cat companion, isn't it? Right here."

Emily nodded and transferred the whole of Peanut's

body into Crystal's arms. A frightened expression flicked onto her face, then was gone. "My goodness. He actually holds some weight."

"Perhaps you have more of a gift than you give yourself credit for," Emily said, chucking the cat under the chin until Peanut's eyes closed with pleasure. "I think he likes you."

"That cat likes anybody," Cynthia said, walking up behind Emily. "It's been a very disappointing discovery to make when I thought he fancied me above all others."

Peanut wriggled in Crystal's arms, clambering awkwardly out of her grip and jumping over to Cynthia's. The smile on his owner's face was beatific.

"Do you feel any different?" Emily asked. "Now that you know what happened at the end?"

The ghost shrugged and screwed up her nose. "Not really. Apart from being glad that it wasn't my family. I would've felt even worse if Nathaniel or Gregory had bumped me off."

"I suppose I meant more in a metaphysical sense."

"A meta-what-now?" Crystal asked.

"If you're referring to the large pool of light currently in my bedroom, which is exerting a strong pull for me to walk towards it, then yes? I think my spirit is now able to move on and my soul is at peace or whatever else it means." She held Peanut up to her nose and breathed in deeply.

Emily hadn't smelled any odour when holding him but wondered if, as two ghosts, Cynthia found the same.

"Do you want to come and see me off?"

Emily nodded. Her throat was tighter than normal, and she found it hard to swallow. "That would be lovely."

"What are we doing?" Crystal said, tugging on Emily's sleeve as she followed Cynthia along the hallway.

"We're going to escort Cynthia onto another plane of

existence. Or something like that," she hastened to add, realising she really had no idea.

"Fantastic!" Crystal beamed and clapped her hands together in excitement. When they walked into the master bedroom, her mouth dropped open in awe. "The light!"

"I really hope this doesn't hurt," Cynthia said, sounding more unsure than Emily had ever heard her.

"You can always jump back out," she said in a firm voice. "It's not like it's a lake of burning fire."

"As if you know." Cynthia cuddled Peanut to her so tightly he gave a frustrated meow. "Wish me luck."

"Good luck," Emily said, and a second later Crystal echoed the sentiment.

Cynthia straightened her back, took a deep breath, walked into the light...

And was gone.

"If I say so myself, that's a job well done." Crystal grabbed hold of Emily's hand as the light faded away to show the unkempt bedroom. "Now, let's go down to the pub or something to celebrate. I'm not sure what the drink of choice is for sending a restless spirit off to her final resting place, but I'm betting it comes with bubbles."

"I think that's a fine idea," Emily said, reaching out to grab her friend's hand.

CHAPTER TWENTY-SIX

*E*mily slid a packet of cigarettes across the counter to Pete. "I don't really wish to encourage your habit, but I wanted to get you something you'd enjoy, and this is the only thing I know for sure you like."

Pete picked up the pack, turning it over to check the brand—almost entirely obscured by a close-up picture of a diseased mouth. "Thank you, I guess. What's this about? You don't need to buy my smokes when I can afford them myself."

"I'm sorry about our fight the other day. It made me feel dreadful, and I didn't want it hanging between us. I should've found a better way to broach the subject."

Her co-worker pushed back from the counter, dragging a stool close enough to sit. When he glanced back up at her, his face was tinged with pink. "I'm the one should be apologising to you about that, I think." He turned the cigarette packet over and over in his hands, flicking his thumb at the tab in the cellophane. "Your case workers called after you left that afternoon, while I was still upset. I told them a lot of stuff I'd normally keep to myself."

"Yeah." Emily gave a rueful grin. "If it makes you feel better, they already brought it up during our meeting and I survived."

"And I was in the wrong as it turned out."

"Neither of us knew that for sure at the time."

"Hey, stop it." Pete held up his hand. "I'm now trying to apologise to you. It just makes it harder when you're so nice about everything."

"It was easier for me to see the connection, is all I meant." Emily leaned on the counter and flexed the back muscle in her leg. She couldn't stand for much more than a few minutes without it trying to contract. "Sariah was just some woman I'd met for the first time. You had a relationship going back a few years."

Pete nodded, his lips curled into a glum expression. "I really hate it when I see the best in people, and it turns out to be a sham."

"It's better to look for the best and be wrong than always assume other people are horrible."

That raised a small smile. "Anyway, we got a large deposit of funds into the charity account this morning, so I need to thank you for that. I'll sort out the commission once the bank clears the payment and transfer it to you."

Emily took a deep breath. "You don't need to do that."

"Why not? It's yours. You earned it and more."

"The caseworker meeting made it pretty clear I won't be able to perform this work for much longer."

Pete shook his head, jutting out his chin. "You don't want to listen to those Debbie Downers."

"Even if I last a few more years, I still need to have a backup plan in place." Emily touched his hand. "It's no good me having all the information then still being surprised when the time comes. I'd rather get something sorted out now."

"So, you're leaving?" Pete chewed on the edge of his bottom lip. "You only just got here."

"I'm not leaving. Not until I can't manage those stairs, at any rate. I just mean I need to sort out an alternate income, so the charity might as well benefit from the work I can do here in the meantime." She glanced over her shoulder at the woman's shelter signage on the door. "I have a few ideas on how to get a new gig going pretty quickly and until then, I've always got the compensation money going into the bank every month."

"You're sure?" Pete put the ciggies away in his jean pocket and leaned forward. "The organisation was pretty clear they're happy to work on the commission structure because the time spent on auctioning the antiques we find, brings in more money overall." He gave a short laugh. "Those boxes mostly just sit upstairs, otherwise. I don't have time to go through them or the eye to know what they're worth."

"I'm happy to keep doing the work. The only reason I have an eye for it is antiquing was my hobby for years. If I can help out now with that skill, all the better. I figure it's about time I put some good vibes out into the world, and this is the easiest way I know how."

"If you change your mind..."

Emily nodded. "I'll let you know if I need the money. I'm not about to starve myself or get turfed out of a home." She tapped her fingers on the counter. "Actually, there is something I want to do out of the funds coming through today if you don't mind."

"Of course, not." Pete stood up again, moving over to the computer when Emily's eyes flicked its way.

"It might sound a bit strange, but I'd like to buy a Magnolia tree for somebody. A woman I know planted one in her son's memory then lost it through a gardening... Um... Misadventure."

"Tell me the address and you can consider it done."

While Emily was reciting Mabel Thistledrop's address, the bell over the door tinkled and Gregory walked inside the store.

"I thought about what you said last night, and I think you're right," he said to Emily.

She'd said and done so much in the last day, it took her a moment to work out to which statement he was referring. "You're volunteering?"

"If you'll have me." Gregory looked suddenly unsure, eyes flicking between Emily and Pete. "I not only got kicked out of school with the drug thing, but I also got fired from my last job. Will that stop me?"

Pete gave the young man one of his broadest, gap-toothed grins. "Not on your life. We believe strongly in second chances here, mate. That's why everything here is second-hand."

At midday, Gregory walked Emily along to the Honey-suckle Café. She had made an appointment for lunch with Crystal the night before and hoped she hadn't been too far into her cups to remember. The medium really liked a drink.

"You can tell me to mind my own business," Emily began.

Gregory gave a groan and a laugh. "That's an ominous way to start a conversation."

"Sorry. I just wondered how you got involved with the prescription drugs. It doesn't seem to fit with your personality."

"It was all the fault of a car," Gregory said. "At least, that's the inanimate object I've chosen to lay all the blame upon. There was an old yellow VW bug that I desperately wanted to buy when I was at Uni. It fitted perfectly with the persona I was trying to establish."

Emily remembered well how much thinking had gone into the personality she displayed to the other students in her own university days. It might have been more decades ago than she liked to remember, but the intense desire to establish herself as an individual still shone bright.

"And your dad didn't want to fund it?" she asked, guessing what was coming.

"No, he didn't. He kept pointing out that the reason he paid money into my Metrocard was because the buses in Christchurch were easy to use and plentiful."

They waited at a pedestrian crossing for a break in the traffic. "It still seems a leap, to go from wanting a car to dealing drugs on campus."

"It wasn't my idea. Some other students had mentioned they used Ritalin to study. I thought it was worth a shot asking Dr Attica when I had a check-up. Neither Mum nor Dad used him, so it wasn't like he'd go telling tales. I assumed he'd just send me packing and warn me of the dangers of misusing pills, but he gave me a script and told me he'd cut me a commission if I brought in more students."

"My goodness." Emily shook her head. "It's hard to believe he'd be that careless."

"It wasn't like I'd gone to him with clean hands," Gregory said with a shrug. "The terms I used might have been different, but I basically asked him to sell me drugs. If he'd gone to the police, it might never have turned into charges but it sure would have got me into strife at home."

"And what happened when he was caught out?"

"Dad wouldn't buy me a car, but he bought me out of trouble quick enough. I think he paid the doctor to formulate some dodgy story and Dr Attica took advantage because he faced even worse penalties than me."

"And Hilda listened in to all of it," Emily said in a low tone as they reached the café.

"I guess so. She was always there, so she must have heard a lot of things we probably shouldn't have discussed in front of her. It's funny how I'd never talk about stuff like this in front of a stranger but..."

Gregory shrugged and Emily nodded. But an old woman just fades into the woodwork. After a while, it's like they're not even there.

"Did you want to join me and Crystal for lunch?" Emily held open the café door.

The young man shook his head. "No. I'll pick something up from the tea rooms on the way back. I just wanted to make sure you got here okay."

He walked away, whistling as he swung his arms in time to his lazy stride. Emily shook her head, feeling older than her years. A nice gesture but, boy did it hurt to be reminded she struggled to walk down the street on her own.

Crystal was seated inside and waved to Emily as she walked into the room. Large windows overlooked the main road with its constant run of traffic. Opposite, a car park outside the tea rooms had a man in a truck splitting his sandwich with a dog seated on the roof.

The medium followed Emily's gaze and laughed. "I sure hope he remembers his friend's perched up there when he takes off."

"I've been thinking," Emily said later, as their meals arrived.

"Sounds dangerous."

"Would you like to go into business together?"

The pause and scrutiny that followed made Emily want to shrink into a tiny ball. But she was done with not being seen. She had a gift, a limited timeframe during which she might be able to use it, and a desire to do some good in the world.

She straightened her back and met Crystal's gaze. "It's okay to say if you don't want a partner. I know you've built up your business from scratch by yourself and bring a lot more to the table than I do."

"Yes."

"If you want to think about it, that's okay, too."

"I said, yes. Let's do it."

"Really?" Emily sat back in her chair, unable to stop a wide smile from blooming on her face. "You're interested."

"Interested. Agreed. Sold." Crystal framed a headline with her hands. "I can see the ads now. Ghost seer and solver of cold case murders."

"I hardly think Cynthia was a cold case. They hadn't even got around to putting up her headstone, she was that fresh."

"If her body was buried, and the police had closed the case, I'm calling it."

Emily poked at her salad, spearing a cherry tomato on her fork. "Are you sure people won't just laugh at us?"

"Not at all. They laugh at me all the time, and I've survived so far. Besides, there's a bloke down the road at Pinetar Beach who's hung out his shingle as a wizard for hire. If he can do that, I'm sure we'll be fine to get our operation off the ground."

They continued to talk as they finished off their meals. By the time Emily walked back into the charity shop, she was flushed with excitement at the possibilities.

Walking up the path to her front door that evening, she wondered how it would be the first time somebody openly laughed at what she was doing. A jolt of anxiety spiked up her back, then Emily shook her head.

"It can't be any worse than when the police laughed in my face," she whispered.

True enough. Her smile was back in place as she walked through to the lounge... and stopped dead in her tracks.

"Peanut?"

The cat lay curled on the cushion where Emily most liked to sit. His sides moved up and down with the rhythm of his breathing. At first glance, he appeared so much like his live self that she clutched a hand to her chest. Then, she saw the way his tail disappeared into the throw cushion.

Ghost cat.

The perfect pet for somebody who might soon struggle to look after herself, let alone another living being.

With cautious movements, Emily sat on the sofa and reached out to stroke Peanut's head. The faintest sensation of touch—a ghostly echo of the real thing—ran through her hand. After a moment, the cat yawned and looked sleepily at his new mistress.

"Thank you," Emily whispered.

Chances were that Cynthia had been and gone long ago, but if she was still close enough to hear, Emily wanted her to know she was grateful.

"Thank you for everything, Mrs Pettigrew."

ABOUT THE AUTHOR

Katherine Hayton is a middle-aged woman who works in insurance, doesn't have children or pets, can't drive, has lived in Christchurch her entire life, and currently resides a two-minute walk from where she was born.

For some reason, she's developed a rich fantasy life.

www.katherinehayton.com

Printed in Great Britain
by Amazon

47831658R00135